"Indiana Jones meets Eckhart Tolle? Yes, indeed! Wow! Where to begin to congratulate you on this extraordinary, cutting-edge, landmark book? It is immensely clever . . . a book that will be referred to in years to come . . . a turning point in the collective psyche. Wow again!"

— **Meg Robinson**, author of *Drawn by a Star*; artist and
philanthropist; healing-art journeys, Andalucía, Spain

"I am an avid reader and read all types of books, so it is rare to have a novel really reach out and move me in a 'big' way. This is a page-turner that hooks you in from the beginning because it is such a great story! It has drama, love, revenge, and resolution. I found myself reading late into the night, wondering what would come next."

— **Janice Staub**, BA, CIM, president, Yaletown Financial
Management and CEO Hyvetown Music

"From the opening pages, the reader is enthralled by a unique and imaginative concept, accompanied by vivid descriptions, and characters we can all relate to. The believable storyline is enhanced by poignant historic references, leaving one wanting to learn and explore more about our human possibilities. Since reading One Great Year, I have noticed a heightened sense of awareness to the energies that surround us. This is a brilliant book. . . . It's going to make a great movie!"

— **Phil McGrew**, Clearwater, BC

"One Great Year grabs you from the get-go and won't let you loose. . . . This is an all-encompassing adventure we are all on. . . . You will land inspired . . . your feet more firmly on your own true path."

— **Prema Lee Gurreri**, author of *Your Sacred Wealth Code*,
and life-purpose mentor, Seattle WA

"The book cannot be put down. I read through the night and could so connect to the characters. There is no doubt in my mind this will be made into a most amazing movie."

—**Hetty Driessen**, Theta Healing Institute of Knowledge,
Urubamba, Peru

WITHDRAWN

The One Great Year Series

Book I

Library of Congress Control Number: 2018948752

Printed in the USA

First Printing, 2018

ISBN-13: 978-1-947637-72-6 print edition
ISBN-13: 978-1-947637-73-3 ebook edition

Waterside Press
2055 Oxford Ave
Cardiff, CA 92007
www.waterside.com

The One Great Year Series

Book I

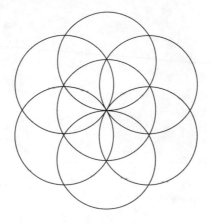

ɛ∽ a Novel by ∾ɞ

Tamara Veitch & Rene DeFazio

Waterside Press
Cardiff-by-the-Sea, CA

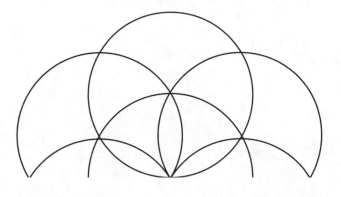

"Life will give you whatever experience is most helpful for the evolution of your consciousness."

— Eckhart Tolle

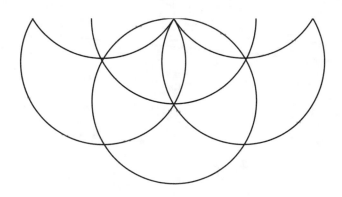

Dedicated to Max, Quinn, Andy, and
all of those who have loved us on our path.

Chapter 1

The Weary Traveler

Present day, Seattle, Washington

Quinn had been reincarnated an exhausting number of times. How many lives had he lived? He could hardly count them. Over the past thirteen thousand years, he had lived through a Golden Age, descended into a Silver Age and a Bronze Age, and then agonized as humanity declined, into the brutal Iron Age.

Plato had called it the "Great Year," and Quinn knew the ancient concept well. Roughly every twenty-six thousand years, the tilted Earth rotated once on its axis, and within that time period there was a rise and fall of consciousness on the planet. Quinn carefully watched the precession of the equinoxes, charting the four Ages of the Great Year Cycle. The star constellations were a cosmic clock, and he had mapped them in all of his lifetimes, awaiting a worldwide awakening.

Throughout the Ages, he had been embroiled in the messy, fickle aspects of life: living, dying, and living again. He had suffered more than most, but unlike other people, Quinn understood why he'd suffered. Still, he longed for a time when all misery would end.

Quinn was different from the rest of humanity; he was special—one of the chosen—but his connection to his purpose was waning. He spent hours every day tracking other Atitalans—Emissaries like himself from the ancient land. They had been sent to guide humankind in its evolution; and many were healers, musicians, scientists, artists, and teachers. They were the way-showers, laying clues for those who would reawaken as the Great Year ascended once again. He clung to the hope that the most difficult time in his obligation was over, give or take a few hundred years.

Emissaries glowed with a distinct indigo shine that set them apart from the auras of other people and differentiated them like fingerprints. He could never identify fellow Emissaries for certain until he saw them in person, because shine was rarely captured in photos and video. If the karmic code did show up, the shot was usually discarded as overexposed. In person, however, even though their bodies and faces were changed, Quinn could recognize his fellow Atitalans immediately. Seeing shine was no special skill—he just knew what to look for. In the Dark Age, the human brain rejected 90 percent of what the eyes saw, but Quinn knew *how* to see.

The Emissary rubbed his forehead with the back of his thumb, ruffling his messy black hair. He lit a joint and searched the night sky. He took a few puffs. It helped to slow the constantly spinning filmstrip of his mind. He brushed a flake of ash from his Lenny Kravitz T-shirt and opened the window a crack, exhaling into the cool Pacific Northwest evening.

The bachelor rented a small apartment in the outer suburbs of Seattle. The forested hills and fields filled him with peace. He watched a bulbous black spider outside his window repair its web. He had watched it climb—trap and mend, over and over, up and down the delicate grid. Quinn observed the microcosm and knew it was a model for understanding the universe: create, destroy, repeat. He felt stuck, like a fly trapped and bound in the most dense and sticky time of the Great Year Cycle. He reminded himself it wouldn't always be like this . . . it hadn't always been like this.

Philosophy, exploration, rebellion—Quinn had done it all, but now he was tired of trying so hard. He was an old soul, and was weighed down by the memories of all his lives before. He pushed away the voice reminding him that lessons remained to be learned. He had to rise up, in spite of the Age.

At fifteen, Quinn had moved in with his bachelor uncle when his mom, a single parent, had been killed in an auto accident. Barely a decade older than his nephew, the man was ill prepared to deal with a child, and by seventeen, Quinn was on his own. Now turning forty-five, sex was easy but love eluded him. He had no girlfriend, no wife. He had only his buddy Nate and a few casual friends. The blogger had chosen a career that kept him anonymous and in the background. Though his blog had a huge following, he warily avoided recognition and notoriety, ever on the lookout for his adversary, Helghul. Helghul had shine too, but unlike the Emissaries' shine, his appeared as a dark shadow around him, flowing with wicked intentions.

The television flickered, and after a moment, Quinn snapped it off in disgust. He tossed the remote onto the chaotic pile of multilanguage newspapers and books that buried his sofa. Gossip and propaganda were pasted like wallpaper over the truths that begged for attention underneath. Fear-mongering egos monopolized the information feed, and consumers ate it up and grew fat on it, ever hungry for more. Dark souls absorbed the spotlight, and chaos had overtaken the planet, but the Emissary knew that suffering had a way of waking the soul.

Thousands of years earlier, in Atitala, Quinn's name had been Marcus, and his Marcus-brain—a deep, ancient consciousness—was awake within him, constantly guiding, educating, and urging him to duty. As the world and humanity continued to falter and crumble around him, he had to rebuild and set an example. In his lifetime as Quinn, he felt sadly inadequate. He assumed that the other Emissaries were active and contributing. He was confident that they were not sedentary, disgruntled, and stoned.

They don't have past-life memories tormenting them, Quinn justified to himself, though he knew he wouldn't give up his memories, even if he could. He took a hard final drag of his tiny roach.

What the hell am I doing with all my memories? Suffering, he thought as he flicked the dying ember and dropped the scrap in a soda can. A frown turned the corners of his mouth, and deep furrows carved his handsome brow. Fatigue caused an ache in his back and neck. It was literally the weight of the world on his shoulders, a world that didn't own its shit.

The Emissary positioned himself in front of his keyboard and began typing his blog. He was determined to reach the public in a way they would welcome. He trusted that his words would reach those who needed it. Hopefully, he was contributing to the ever-evolving collective consciousness. His compulsion to expose humankind to the truths surrounding them would not be denied.

Quinn had tried to ignore the obligation that dogged him. In this life, as in all his lives, he had traveled the world searching for an elusive spirit, one he loved deeply beyond all others. Despite his searching, Theron had not been found—not this time, not yet.

Chapter 2

Marcus, Theron, and Helghul

11,600 BCE, Atitala

Atitala was an advanced civilization and the seat of power to a nation that stretched across the Atlantic. The central unitary was led by White Elder and a Senate of seven additional Elders.

The Elders were enlightened masters who incarnated on Earth in specific roles to help humankind in its evolution, though they, too, would eventually evolve beyond these roles and be replaced by their students.

The eight Elders were named after the colors between light and its absence. There was: Green, Red, Yellow, Blue, Orange, and

Grey Elder, as well as Black and White. Each color corresponded to the role the Elders fulfilled in service of their people.

Only Black Elder was enigmatic, known solely through historical references. In Atitala, no one but the Elders had ever seen him, nor had they hoped to. Black Elder was not a part of life in the Golden Age, for he was most powerful in the darkest times, and he was unable to function within a democratic, united Senate. He would someday return to reprise his role in the world, emphasizing the needs of the individual and heightening the selfish desire for power and control over others. In so doing, he would highlight the importance of choice in the soul's evolution.

Black Elder's role was the opposite of that of White Elder. White Elder embodied empathy, compassion, unconditional love, and the aspiration to return to the light. She was loved and admired by her people.

It was here among these teachers that Marcus was born into the Golden Age. Both of his parents had died before his seventh year—a theme often repeated in his lives—but Marcus had chosen them well. In their short time together, they had demonstrated unconditional love; and their genetic legacy had ensured he was creative, intelligent, and healthy. In this enlightened Age, lifetimes were long and death was not feared; it was an accepted transition, but Marcus missed his parents just the same.

Upon their passing, Marcus had gone to live with Helghul, and *his* mother and father. As Marcus had grown, he and Helghul had been the best of friends. It comforted him that though he had lost the people he loved most, he had the companionship of his best buddy. The boys were near the same age and had been inseparable since speaking their first words. Even though they looked like opposites, with Helghul being fair of skin, eyes, and hair, while Marcus was dark, their personalities had complemented each other perfectly. When building with blocks, at the tender of age four, they had piled alternately, perfectly, in time and balance, easily creating a massive tower in unison, as if their four hands were of one brain.

The boys had known Theron since they were toddlers, and she had gravitated toward them naturally. As they had matured, their attachment had become firmly established, and they were rarely seen apart.

By age thirteen, Helghul and Theron were well developed and pubescent, while Marcus was a late bloomer who remained skinny, hairless, and small. Helghul didn't seem to notice his advantage over his friend; instead, he appreciated Marcus's loyal and humble manner.

Existence in Atitala had been peaceful and predictable for millennia, but daily life was becoming more complicated as emotions grew increasingly volatile and individuals became more self-centered. As an example, the teens were discussing a troubling interaction they had just witnessed in the marketplace. There was no monetary system in Atitala. The citizens relied on barter and goodwill exchanges of goods and services, and the students had been surprised to hear a young cloth seller in an argument with a patron.

"I require more in exchange."

"But this is what we agreed to."

"Go to the stall down the way. I have told you what I want," they heard.

It was remarkable that the seller did not offer an amicable solution. Marcus, Theron, and Helghul were discussing the transaction as they walked through a grassy courtyard when ahead they saw four Elders dwarfed by a particularly pale and lanky visitor nearly twice their height. The unprecedented sight quickly made them forget the marketplace.

"Who's that?" Helghul asked, excited by the possibility of a mystery. He was bored by the predictable daily tasks that held the interest of his fellow students, and despite often being restless, he hid his discontent.

"A Lemurian!" Marcus deduced, noticing the man's long, delicate fingers and skin that shimmered blue due to the purple veins visible through his translucent skin.

"It must be the Willowy Man!" Theron whispered. She had heard her mother, White Elder, mentioning him the night before, in strangely hushed tones.

The Willowy Man was legendary in Atitala though he had never visited in their lifetime. He was the Tunnel-Keeper, facilitating between the realms of Inner and Outer Earth and navigating the ley lines, also known as fire lines, by way of the electric currents within the Earth's magma.

The young ones stared, wide-eyed and curious.

"Strange that he should venture to Outer Earth. I wonder why he's here. It must be something important," Theron said.

Helghul moved closer to listen, and Theron followed while Marcus lagged behind. The smaller boy admired his daring friends for their confidence, but his nature was more reserved.

White, Grey, Yellow, and Red Elder were in deep discussion with Willowy Man but noticed the youngsters and permitted them to listen and observe. The innate wisdom and creativity of children was highly valued in Atitala, and the Elders encouraged them to contribute should they have something insightful to add. Great things were expected of Marcus, Theron, and Helghul, and it was synchronistic that the three brightest learners among the young should pass by at that moment.

"The Tunnel-Keeper is rightly concerned," Yellow Elder said gravely. Despite being aged and frail in appearance, Yellow Elder embodied the warrior energy. In the Golden Age, strength was demonstrated philosophically, not by brute force.

"The fall is imminent," said Grey Elder. He was the Elder of architecture and mathematics, responsible for teaching the design of the universe and its ever-fluid balance.

"I must begin moving the atlantium back to Inner Earth," Willowy Man said solemnly.

"It will be a powerful blow to everyone living in Atitala," White Elder said.

Atlantium crystal was mined in Inner Earth and was a power source that created free, inexhaustible, clean energy by harnessing the Earth's magnetic field. It allowed the holder to control gravity and movement and provided all of the power to the city. It was responsible for miraculous advances in flight and was used in the building of all the great architectural structures in Atitala, including the perfectly designed White Pyramid.

"Life in Atitala will be profoundly different without atlantium," Red Elder said. As a historian, scribe, and the official Keeper of the Records, Red Elder would note the significance of losing the crystal and document its date in the Halls of Amenti. Atlantium was an essential tool in the Golden Age. The youngsters listened in rapt silence, their heads spinning with the ramifications of that change.

"We will return the atlantium and honor our agreement with the Inner Earthlings," said White Elder.

"Perhaps it can be delayed; we don't know how quickly things will decline," Yellow Elder suggested.

"The request to return the atlantium comes from the Inner Earth Council," said White Elder. "We will honor it. The decline has grown increasingly evident. The fall may come sooner and more suddenly than expected."

"What of the Emerald Tablet?" Grey Elder asked, referring to the most sacred and powerful artifact in Atitala. It was made of solid atlantium and was imbued with wisdom that gave it properties and abilities far beyond a simple shard.

"The Emerald Tablet will remain in your care," said Willowy Man.

"We will protect your generous gift," White Elder assured him.

"May the Tablet's light guide your people in the darkening," said Willowy Man.

White Elder turned to Theron and her friends. "Have you any questions? Anything to add?" she asked.

Theron struggled to offer something meaningful, but she felt only concern about the coming changes, and this "low level" thinking was far from anything she wanted to share with her enlightened mother.

"Why must the atlantium be moved?" Helghul asked.

"The technology must be protected. As the Great Year descends, consciousness will decline. As people and civilization grow darker, the atlantium could be used to destroy the living planet," Yellow Elder replied. The lines mapping his face rested softly, with no sign of stress.

"Our way of life and level of conscious awareness will be devastated and forgotten," White Elder said.

"Atitala will be destroyed?" Theron asked, visibly alarmed.

"Eventually all things change from one form into another," White Elder continued calmly.

Theron admired the serenity of her mother's countenance but couldn't match it. *Destroyed! Atitala will be destroyed! How can she be so composed?* Theron thought. Once again she had failed to act as her mother did, though it was Theron's ever-pressing goal to do so.

"What if it doesn't have to be that way?" Helghul interjected, turning to Willowy Man. The visitor had been listening carefully and had, without bias, formed an impression of the trio.

"What do you propose?" Willowy Man asked, pleased with the discourse.

"Use the fire lines!" Marcus and Helghul said in unison. If one had the expertise, telluric currents could be accessed and traveled at incredible speed, from Inner to Outer Earth, belying the illusion of material solidity. They knew it was the knowledge of these currents that allowed the Tunnel-Keeper to travel through solid stone from Outer to Inner Earth.

"If you can transport the atlantium to Inner Earth for safe-keeping, why not move the people?" Helghul continued.

"If thoughts create reality . . . and we think it possible . . . is it not worth the effort?" Marcus reasoned.

"If manifesting an alternative were possible, the Elders would certainly do so . . . wouldn't you?" Theron asked, looking to her mother. Surely White Elder and the others would have considered every benevolent possibility. They would not surrender Atitala and her citizens carelessly.

"The probability of the Age declining is high, and the Elders are bound to the evolution of consciousness," Willowy Man answered. Marcus studied the Elders, one by one, noticing the calm acceptance in their eyes.

"We are not Elders. So we are not bound," Marcus said, implying that he and his friends could create an alternate outcome despite a low probability of success. Helghul smiled and linked arms with him in solidarity.

"The Ages of the Great Year descend, and your ability to create reality declines with them. You would not be the first to attempt their derailing. One may delay the inevitable, but it certainly remains . . . inevitable," Yellow Elder said. It was clear from Helghul's furrowed brow that he was unconvinced.

"I will begin my task immediately. I am comforted to know Atitala is in capable hands," Willowy Man said, excusing himself and ending any further discussion.

The Elders also adjourned; and Marcus, Helghul, and Theron found shade in a protected knoll to further consider what they had learned.

"You're right, Marcus. The Elders might be bound to honor the decline of the Great Year, but *we* are not," Helghul said.

"Bound to honor it or not, Helghul, you heard Yellow Elder—it's inevitable," Theron argued. "Trying to intervene would be pointless."

"I heard, 'one may delay the inevitable,'" Helghul said slowly, obviously deep in thought. "If we can delay it, then it would be possible to prolong the Golden Age."

"It is highly improbable," Theron said. She knew Helghul well enough to know that the excitement and resolve spinning within him was unstoppable.

"They said they will start moving caches of atlantium through the quarry immediately. We'll conceal ourselves in the atlantium, and Willowy Man will transport us to Inner Earth without realizing," Helghul suggested.

"Then what?" Theron asked, slightly exasperated.

"We try to figure out the fire lines ourselves . . . or we convince the Inner Earthlings to help our people, and we design a plan for an evacuation when the time comes. I don't know what will happen, but we can't just wait for some doomsday to arrive!" Helghul said.

"What if it doesn't work?" Theron asked, her hand now tightly holding Helghul's. Her admiration for him was clear on her face.

"What if it does?" Helghul retorted, glowing.

"It's worth the risk," Marcus said, "but we'll have to get around the Nephilim. They'll never let us pass." He nervously ran his hands through his messy black hair.

The Nephilim were giants who mined the atlantium and were responsible for its movement through the quarry. Children were not allowed near the mines. They had grown up being told that the Nephilim were neither friend nor foe and that they were self-serving, with no allegiance to anyone or anything. It was best to stay far away from them, for they could not be trusted.

"Leave them to me," Helghul said, and the skeleton of an adventure had begun to take shape.

From the grass, the young friends gazed up at the giant banyan limbs shading them and watched the puffy white clouds floating across the blue. They lay in a circle, listening to the hum of the birds and insects, with the crowns of their heads touching. It was the last time they would link arms and lie under the sky of their homeland. Their lives in Atitala would never be the same. The trio had no idea their adventure would set in motion a series of events that would completely alter the people they would become.

Helghul had devised a plan to distract the Nephilim in order to sneak past them. He had remembered a celebration on a distant island where he had witnessed huge multicolored lanterns being released to the skies. He remembered how delighted everyone had been watching the unusual display, and he counted on the release of colorful inflatables creating the same excitement among the Nephilim. He and his friends were up most of the night secretly sewing and gluing the props needed for their plan.

By sunrise they were prepared and under way. They marched into the jungle near the quarry carrying supplies and accompanied by five trustworthy fellow students they had recruited to help. Bapoo, Solenna, Yashoda, Kushim, and Holt understood the magnitude and importance of their caper, and they were honored to be trusted with this task. The allies were crouched in the jungle across the outskirts of the quarry beneath the plateau where the Nephilim transported the atlantium.

"Have you considered a confrontation with the Guardians?" Theron asked.

Helghul had not.

"What if we happen upon one of *those* while we're in there?" she asked as she, Marcus, and Helghul set up their distraction.

"They're not real. They're mythical . . . aren't they?" Marcus asked, stopping his work.

The Guardians were fierce creatures said to guard the boundaries between the realms of Inner and Outer Earth as well as between the material and spiritual realms.

"Oh, they're real. White Elder told me about them," Theron replied.

Marcus pondered the possibility while he unraveled the crimson bundle in his arms.

"We'll deal with them should the time come. We mean no harm. They won't bother us," Helghul said.

Marcus was unconvinced, and beside him, Bapoo listened uneasily, relieved that he was not sneaking into Inner Earth.

"We will have to be alert, but Mother said they wear warning bells around their necks, so we should hear them before we see them," Theron said. A nervous shiver ran through her, and she wiggled to shake it off.

"You think we'll see one?" Marcus asked.

"They travel in pairs," Theron replied.

"Reassuring!" Marcus quipped.

"What if you don't return? What should I do if something goes wrong?" Bapoo asked, suddenly concerned for his friends.

"What if something goes right?" Marcus replied, patting Bapoo on the back with more confidence than he felt.

Helghul smiled upon hearing the optimistic response by his best friend.

The students had cleared spiky barbs of jungle undergrowth and peered through leafy branches from five locations around the quarry. Layers of multicolored silk and long strands of rope were folded in neat piles on the ground at their feet.

"Bapoo, the ropes are secured underneath these rocks. Solenna and the others will cut theirs free when we give the signal," Helghul said, placing a laser on the ground beside the skinny brown boy who looked as though he could have been Marcus's brother.

Marcus observed the sentry on the outcropping above.

"Look at the size of him!" he exclaimed, gesturing toward the Nephilim guarding the entrance.

"Once the inflatables draw all of the Nephilim out of the cave, we won't have long," Helghul noted.

"We're ready to begin filling," Marcus said, tying the last knot and looking up to find Helghul scrutinizing him. Theron was long, lean, and fast like him, but Marcus was slower and might fall behind.

You don't have to worry. I can do this, Helghul, Marcus assured him telepathically. They often used telepathy. It was learned by all Atitalans from infancy. It was an intimate and familiar way of communicating among family members and friends. It was not an unspoken voice—not words, exactly; it was more like intentionally transmitting images, feelings, and meaning.

I know you can, Helghul answered, squeezing his friend's bony shoulder. "We're ready!"

Bapoo began inflating the sphere at his feet. The red silk puffed and billowed, filling up. Bigger and bigger it expanded until one side lifted off the ground, dwarfing the teens. Sturdy brown ropes were secured up each seam and circled under the nearby boulder, anchoring the inflatable to the ground until just the right moment.

"Can you handle it on your own?" Marcus asked. Bapoo looked up, and Marcus saw the beads of sweat developing on his brow.

"Are you sure about this?" Bapoo asked.

"No, I'm not, but if we risk nothing, we accomplish nothing," Marcus said, though thoughts of the Guardians caused his nerves to quaver.

"We told you what the Elders said, Bapoo. Maybe if we figure out the fire lines or convince the Inner Earthlings to help us, Atitala will survive," Theron said.

"But we're just at the end of the Golden Age. Isn't there still time?"

"No. The decline into the Silver Age has started," Marcus said.

"History tells us that the transitional periods are unstable," Theron added.

"Just do your part and we'll do ours," Helghul said, tugging Marcus and Theron by their arms and leading them through the jungle. They climbed up a steep rocky cliff toward the cave entrance. He could see the Nephilim sentry and was careful to stay in his blind spot. If he succeeded in finding a way to save the people of Atitala, Helghul knew he would be a hero. He would rise in status, which could only aid in his bid to someday become White Elder. He came from an honored family; he was strong, intelligent, and ambitious, and great things were expected of him. Helghul felt like something very big was about to unfold.

The three scaled the side of the cave opening and knelt behind a ledge, looking down on the behemoth guarding the entrance. Tufts of hair protruded from random patches on his ears, cheeks, and shoulders, and he stood more than three times the height and width of a human. The giant's balled fists looked like small boulders, and Marcus imagined the crushing blow they could deliver. They were close enough to smell the stench and hear the garbled grunts and exchanges echoing from inside the cavern.

Marcus's stomach was churning. He realized that his breathing had become strained, so he inhaled and exhaled deeply to subdue his angst. It hadn't occurred to any of them to fear the Nephilim. Up until now, he and his friends had lived a fearless life. Suffering and pain were distant concepts, and premature death, though undesirable, was not feared but seen as a new beginning.

"I have no interest in an early rebirth," Marcus whispered.

"You're not going anywhere!" Helghul assured him, though his own thoughts had been less than certain despite his conscious effort to keep them positive.

As Helghul was about to signal for the silk inflatables to be released, a cargo vimana descended from above. Vimanas were the various-sized atlantium-powered transports used in Atitala. Pilots easily harnessed the antigravity properties of atlantium, and flew by sending their intentions into the responsive crystals. The vimana had traversed over the mountain and was lowering onto the platform below them.

"Hide!" Helghul ordered as he pulled Marcus and Theron lower into the crevice. The craft docked, and a door opened to offload a shipment of atlantium.

"This is good," Helghul said. "We can conceal ourselves in those crates."

There were four crates in all, and the open-topped containers allowed the crystals to reflect the sun and shone like emerald beacons on the hillside. They could see the back of the pilot clearly as he waited for the cargo doors to reseal. The students had not been spotted. Theron exhaled in relief as the vehicle departed.

"The one with a head like a gourd seems to be in charge," Helghul whispered. A Nephilim with a long, lumpy face like a butternut squash that had multiple wartlike growths on it was directing two others as they lifted either end of one crate. The leader continued grunting a garbled language and waving toward the corner of the cave.

"He seems agitated," Theron said nervously. She had never been so close to the beastly creatures. She had not realized how enormous and menacing they truly were.

"We don't want to get caught by those things," Helghul said. He hoped things would go smoothly. It occurred to him that he might have steered his best friends into serious trouble. "Get into one of those bins and hide yourself under the atlantium before they carry it into the cave. Use the crystal's antigravity to get in and under it unseen."

"You mean split up?" Marcus asked, not wanting to be separated from his friends.

"We'll never fit together. It would be too obvious," Helghul said.

Marcus knew Helghul was right. There was little that Marcus didn't understand intellectually, but his friends were more daring than he was.

"We can stay connected using telepathy," Theron said.

Marcus and his friends could see the tops of the balloons ready and bobbing, barely visible over the foliage. So far they had counted four Nephilim on the platform.

They had scaled the ridge, staying out of sight, and were poised above the cave entrance. They were a short climb and drop away from their final hiding places when, using a quartz crystal in the sunlight, Helghul signaled their accomplices to release the balloons.

It was a magnificent sight as the five silk balls began lifting from the jungle and speckling the quarry walls with bright dots of red, yellow, green, blue, and orange. The trio waited, adrenaline pumping, for the moment when they would spring, knowing they must be neither seen nor heard.

For a moment it seemed as if the Nephilim might not be baited, but then the sentry turned his gaze to the landscape inquisitively as the balloons rose one by one. They were large and cumbersome, with their brown ropes that caused them to bulge oddly. The sentry was joyfully amused by the awkward-looking inflatables. He called out to the butternut-squash leader, pointing at the demonstration. As the wind pushed and lifted each of the balloons, their silky domes were illuminated by the sun. The gourd-headed giant lumbered forward to investigate, and his steps pounded the Earth.

Ten, eleven, twelve, Theron counted, staring at the cave. More giants curiously emerged, shielding their eyes from the glaring sun. There were twelve Nephilim on the platform; and most were grunting, staring, and pointing in amusement. Only one seemed indifferent and hung back from the ridge, lingering at the cave entrance.

We can't go! That one will see us, Helghul projected. It was no longer safe to whisper. Theron had been watching the holdout, hoping he would move just ten steps forward. That short distance was all they needed to slip behind the giants and into the crates. The diversion would not captivate the others forever.

Just then, the wind gusted, and the single red balloon came nearer, drifting toward them with its brown ropes trailing underneath. The crowd of Nephilim erupted in deep staccato sounds that resembled laughter and multiplied as all work was abandoned. Their grim faces contorting in amusement, the giants implored the wind to bring the large red balloon to them.

The sentry was the closest to the approaching sphere, and he grunted lowly with pleasure as his thick lips revealed crooked yellow teeth. His fellow Nephilim watched from the platform while the sentry leaned precariously over the edge and grabbed hold of the red balloon. He wrapped his bulky hand around the fabric and rope with a celebratory howl. He had expected to reel in his prize, but instead the wind dragged the unstable Nephilim along the dirt and lifted him off his feet. With a gust, he was pulled up and away from his perch, over the edge; his huge gnarled toes kicked and searched for the ground. The crowd reacted in disbelief with a rumble of laughter. The straggler, who had been lingering at the cave entrance, now moved forward to watch his colleague float away, spinning at the mercy of the powerful balloon, toward the jungle. Theron projected thoughts of gratitude to the Air Elementals, who had either intentionally or accidentally helped them.

Go now! Helghul telegraphed to his friends, leaping across the top of the opening and sliding down the curving rock of the entrance, landing on the right side beside the waiting crates and catching Theron and Marcus as they slid to join him. *Get inside quickly!*

They used the atlantium crystals, and with their minds, they shifted and moved the loads easily until they were hidden under a reasonable layer. Helghul had submerged himself last, first ensuring that his friends were properly concealed.

They'll turn around any second! Theron had said to Helghul urgently as he buried himself in crystals of varied sizes.

I'm in, Helghul said. Their hearts were pounding in their ears as they struggled to catch their breath.

It worked! Theron was relieved.

This isn't over yet, Marcus replied. He hoped Theron and Helghul couldn't sense the anxiety he was determined to conceal.

Now, they had only to wait, and in the silence, they wondered what was yet to come.

Outside, the amusement continued for the Nephilim as the sentry was dragged across the jungle, kicking, bobbing, and spinning while he hit high branches, which caused great cheers from his fellow workers. Once over the lake, the awkward hulk released the inflatable and dropped. His body twisted as he flopped, landing with a slap in the water. The callous observers chortled, smacking one another on the back.

Bapoo and the other accomplices had gathered together and watched from the jungle. Up, then down, the giant's arms and legs splashed like thick tree trunks, and then bubbles surged to the surface as the colossus sank. The adolescents grew concerned; this was not the plan. He must not come to harm because of them. They were scrambling to intervene when he slowly emerged, walking upright along the bottom of the lake, and came ashore. Smiling a gruesome, droopy smile, and thoroughly entertained by his adventure, he returned, soaking wet, to his post.

The Nephilim resumed their duties carrying the atlantium into the cave. Unable to mentally harness the antigravity properties of the crystal because their genetic frequency had not yet advanced to the level needed to do so, they instead relied on brute force.

The stowaways were silent as they were jostled, not knowing what was to come or how long it would take. Though they couldn't see it, the surface of the solid wall in front of them had begun subtly vibrating. It created ripples that shifted into different beautiful geometric forms, changing its state of matter and appearing gelatinous and fluid before revealing an opening.

Willowy Man stepped out of the tunnel that had appeared. It was higher and much wider than he was, and the inside looked as though it had melted, with glistening drips and waves that slipped down the walls and appeared liquid. By suspending his hand over top of the open crates, Willowy Man, unlike the Nephilim, was able to easily move the cargo.

Marcus was unnerved, but he couldn't attempt to communicate with his friends, or Willowy Man would certainly perceive it.

Once the waiting crates, including those carrying Marcus, Helghul, and Theron, had been moved within his passageway, the Tunnel-Keeper slowly ran his hands around the walls, sensing which notch or ridge would carry him to his preferred destination. His thin pink lips mouthed a silent ceremonial litany. There were infinite possibilities, but the Tunnel-Keeper's ability to listen through his fingertips allowed him to harness the currents and be propelled through the vortexes to his projected destination.

The Tunnel-Keeper made broad, circular movements, like a maestro orchestrating a symphony. His hands flowed, connecting with a surge of energy from inside the stone, and with a final swipe, the portal closed behind them. Suddenly, like a surfer catching a wave, Willowy Man and his cargo were swept through the rock, in perpetual motion.

The three stowaways concentrated attentively for a sound or mind pictures that might help them learn how Willowy Man utilized the natural electromagnetic telluric currents of the planet, but it was futile.

They were spiraling on waves of energy, riding the looping kaleidoscope of geometric lines. Even within the atlantium, the stowaways were aware of the constant change, light, heat, color, and sound. The unfamiliar experience was unsettling, and they were comforted to be chaperoned by the amiable Lemurian.

Hrrmmph! They set down with a gentle thump. They had arrived in Inner Earth and were currently located far beneath the southernmost continent that would later be known on Outer

Earth as Antarctica. They had landed at the opening of a granite cave. It was one of millions of similar openings in the honeycomb lattice that encircled the sun at the center of Inner Earth. The network of caves was connected by tunnels that led out in layers, reaching rivers of iron, and in the east, butting up against a vast freshwater ocean teeming with unfamiliar creatures.

As Willowy Man grew accustomed to the higher vibration of the Inner Earth, the complexity of the material structures around him became defined. He and his secret human cargo were on the distant outskirts of an extensive settlement, with distinct organization. There were finely honed oval-and-round cavities that rippled in every direction as far as the eye could see, and a bustling community of Inner Earth Dwellers, known as Arya, moved in and out of the openings, floating above the ground rather than walking.

The Arya were graceful, translucent, and humanoid in appearance. Their light-filled bodies cast a glow reminiscent of jellyfish. Their skin was transparent, and under the surface, effervescent blue energy flowed like blood.

The Arya were a subterranean race that had moved underground eons earlier when the atmosphere of Outer Earth had changed and become too oxygen-rich, threatening their existence. To prevent their eventual annihilation by literally burning up, they had accessed and developed the catacombs of Inner Earth. They had escaped extinction and had evolved over millions of years. It was they who had first discovered the properties and uses for atlantium, which they shared with humans of Outer Earth only during Golden Ages.

The Arya were the most peaceful and incorruptible civilization ever known to Earth, and they had enjoyed more than two hundred thousand years of peace. They had evolved beyond material wants and needs but were still a part of the Great Year Cycle, and they were affected by the descent of Atitala and all of Outer Earth into the Dark Ages. They felt it in the same way that people might experience allergies: a foggy, uncomfortable itch—but the threat to Inner Earth was real. The Arya must guard the atlantium during the descending ages so that it could not be used for the destruction of the planet. Iron Age humans could not be trusted.

Willowy Man waited as the atlantium was transferred by the Arya. He nodded gratefully before returning to the fire lines and disappearing to who knows where. The crates, with Marcus, Theron, and Helghul silently in tow, were transported through the extensive tunnels to designated outposts for safekeeping.

Helghul had grown fidgety. They were all tired of waiting and hiding. Finally, once the movers had surely departed, Marcus was the first to communicate.

Are you there? Theron? Helghul?

I'm here, Theron replied.

Helghul? Helghul? they both sent out, but there was no response.

Theron? Marcus? Helghul called mentally. Nothing.

⋙⋘ ⋙⋘ ⋙⋘

Helghul slowly began shifting the atlantium that covered him, aware of the intense heat in the space. Light filtered in from a round opening on the far wall. He was grateful to stretch and fill his senses, but he found that movement awkward, and breathing difficult. As soon as he pushed aside the atlantium that had been concealing him, he began to float into the air. He realized there was no gravity and that the atlantium had been stabilizing him. Helghul saw piles and containers of atlantium within the honeycomb pockets around him. Much of it was raw, in various-sized crystals that were easily adapted for daily use, but other pieces had been fashioned into fire urns, statues, jewelry, and other ceremonial objects. He floated, his feet above his head, hanging on to the crates and moving hand over hand to retrieve atlantium objects that would be helpful. He found two bracelets in a nearby pile, and he donned them as anklets that allowed him to walk in the manner he was accustomed, though with a bounce in his step.

The antigravitational environment was incredibly diverse. Inner Earth was laid out around a central sun. Long, equidistant tunnels led out from the sun, and smaller branches ran between rings of granite and nickel caves that spiraled in a circular pattern. The tafoni structure was made up of millions of deep and shallow hollows and rooms that were linked by ribbons of curving passageways. Massive white crystal feldspar deposits stood like forests and illuminated grey-quartz and black-mica crystal towers. Molten iron flowed in rivers through underground channels, and the humidity from the expansive freshwater ocean was unbearably high. The temperature was brutally hot, and strange colorful beasts roamed and soared, surviving alongside the Arya on the shores of the lush, green seaside. Unusual disc-shaped vimanas zipped through the air above.

Helghul had been delivered a good distance from Marcus and Theron. He had walked closer to the center of the complex toward the glow of the sun, while the others had unwittingly begun moving toward the outer boundaries.

Helghul discovered countless atlantium-filled chambers as he searched for his friends, planning how they would approach their hosts to convince them to help save the inhabitants of Atitala.

It was growing hotter, and as Helghul got closer to the center of Inner Earth, he found it harder to breathe. The straight tunnel had grown wider than any he had seen thus far, and the light radiating from the end compelled him to get closer. Helghul was amazed and confused by what he saw as he neared. The passage was lined with Arya. They were oblivious to his presence; he did not understand that they were absorbed in a regenerative daily feeding. It was eerie to see them as they floated immobile above the ground, their eyes closed and their faces basking in the life-giving light.

There were thousands of Arya with their backs to him. He was moving cautiously, wondering how to approach them and ask for help, when he received a clear telepathic message: *Do not disturb them*, it warned.

Helghul froze, engulfed by a powerful wave of fear that was alien to him. A shadowy figure shifted behind him; it had been following his every move.

I have awaited your arrival, Helghul, the stranger said telepathically. His handsome black face was difficult to make out in the diffused light, but his eyes were bright and focused; he was human. Helghul's throat and chest constricted, and his heart swelled with rapid, panicked beating. Terror gripped him, and his intuition prickled his skin, washing him in chills. He was feeling intense fear for the first time in his life, and his mind and body revved in confusion as he struggled to identify the stranger, to calm his rush of emotion, and to decipher the intuitive jolt.

Who are you? Helghul asked, feigning fearlessness and wishing to rid himself of the uncomfortable feelings. He wanted, more than anything, to appear confident and brave, but he also wanted to run.

Helghul's distress was plain to the intruder, who was taking the ill-mannered liberty of accessing the boy's thoughts without permission. Helghul unsuccessfully tried to expel the man from his mind, but the stranger continued shuffling through, causing him to squirm uncomfortably.

I am Black Elder, he replied.

Helghul was shocked by the revelation, and it expanded his fear rather than appeasing it. He looked past the Elder; his passageway was blocked. He would either run directly into the mass of feeding Arya, or into the formidable force before him.

Ahhh, yes. I see your confusion, your turmoil. Certainly a child born into a Golden Age cannot understand. It is fear that you are feeling. An emotion among others that you will know well in the coming Ages. You are wise to be frightened of things you don't understand, but you needn't fear me. It is my endeavor and privilege to inform you that your destiny is, at this moment, in your grasp.

What do you know about my destiny? Helghul asked.

You've come here to help your people, but you need to think bigger. You've always known you would become an Elder. You're in a position to help humanity understand what it means to be human. To question their lives beyond the beliefs they will come to fight and kill for. To question the philosophies and ideologies that will divide people.

How can I do that? I have no experience with such things, Helghul insisted.

Black Elder placed his hand on Helghul's chest. Helghul flinched but was unable to break away from the powerful pull of the Elder's prana that was now coursing through him.

Can you feel that power surging through you? Black Elder asked.

A primal grunt escaped Helghul and echoed off the cave walls. The fear that had inundated the boy was gone, and he felt a rush of confidence and security as the stranger's shine filled him. Snaking ribbons of dark energy wrapped around Helghul, looping in and out, and eclipsing the boy's fair shine completely. He felt an overwhelming sense of confirmation, and he realized that he was perfect and immensely powerful. He was a far cry from the guileless thirteen-year-old boy of moments before, and he wanted it to last—forever.

Who sent you? Helghul asked. He was awestruck, and alternately glanced from Black Elder's face to his own hands. He was stunned that he could feel so completely transformed and still be the same young man.

It is you who has been sent. I have been waiting for the one who would come. I am from an Age long past. As Black Elder, I became more important and more powerful than White Elder. In the coming Ages, you can too.

I can? Helghul thought, still vibrating with the feelings of invincibility imparted by the interloper's touch.

You are the brightest and the best of your Age. You have the ability to attain the stature few can.

Helghul was excited to be recognized and singled out. He knew he was destined for greatness. He always had—everyone did—but now this incredible presence confirmed it. The strength he felt was further inflamed by every prideful thought. His reverie was interrupted by the faces of Marcus and Theron flashing through his mind.

"I have to find my friends," Helghul said with an authority that surprised him. He had switched from telepathic to verbal communication to create more distance between himself and the stranger. He bravely pushed passed the cloaked man and away from the feeding Arya, but the Elder followed patiently.

"They will only hold you back, *Tyro*," Black Elder said, using the customary title for an apprentice and speaking aloud for the first time. His voice was melodic and smooth. "I was once like you, filled with the worries of others. That was before I became the greatest leader Outer Earth has ever known. I have now evolved beyond my human incarnations, and it is you who is meant to take my place as Black Elder. You will lead the world in the coming Ages."

Helghul stopped; he wanted to believe. His body continued to vibrate with a magnificent sense of importance that spiked and tingled with every lofty promise. He aspired to be the top Elder. The idea of being more powerful than White Elder was appealing. Helghul was intoxicated by all of the new emotions gripping him.

"What must I sacrifice?" Helghul asked bravely, bolstered by Black Elder's shared energy and thrilled at the prospect of becoming a leader.

"You will sacrifice only the part of yourself that will prevent you from becoming great."

"What is that?" Helghul asked, searching the Elder's dark face.

"Your empathy," Black Elder answered with a dismissive shrug.

Helghul looked perplexed. Black Elder had begun circling him, and the young man twisted to keep him in view.

"Have you ever seen the Elders act from emotion? In all situations they are able to remain level and calm. You will maintain your ability to love and to feel other emotions, but the weakness of empathy merely distracts you from your personal journey and ambition."

Still imbued with Black Elder's shine, Helghul felt stronger and more powerful than he had ever thought possible, and he wanted it to continue. Everything Black Elder said made sense and excited him.

Black Elder continued to speak. "You may choose to linger and suffer through the descending Ages in your bid to rise at some distant time as White Elder, though there is no guarantee that you will be chosen. I offer you a guarantee. You can choose to take my place. Your incarnations will be significant, evolving humanity and consciousness."

Helghul reflected on the offer. "I have to think," he said. What would happen if he relinquished his empathy? Helghul reveled in the power surging through him. He contemplated what it would mean to become Black Elder—to embrace the whispered reality of the Dark Ages and rise during them rather than shrink. The dark times were so far gone that to Helghul they seemed unreal. The boy had never contemplated any role other than White Elder, but now his options had doubled, and the indeterminate wait had been eliminated altogether.

"My touch not only quelled your fear; it disclosed to you what greatness you can achieve. However, the empowered state you are experiencing is a temporary gift," Black Elder said once again, placing his palm on the center of Helghul's chest.

With a sudden lurch, Helghul felt as though the hand had reached deep inside of him, to the pit of his stomach. The fist took hold, wrenching his guts, tearing away the power pulsing within him and leaving him depleted.

Black Elder lowered his hand, and Helghul stumbled forward. He was returned to his former self, and though he no longer feared Black Elder, he felt weak. His discontent was immediate. A mere child in the shadow of this strange force, he trembled with uncertainty at the energy's withdrawal.

"Bring it back!" Helghul said, desperate to once again feel the intoxicating supremacy of Black Elder's shine surging through him.

"You can bring it back permanently, should you have the courage, but this task is not for the weak," Black Elder said, pulling something from the folds of his robe.

Helghul recoiled. The man now held a long, silver dagger.

He's going to kill me! Helghul thought, raising his arms to protect himself.

"Take it," Black Elder said, holding out the knife.

Helghul took the weapon hesitantly, his hands shaking, and he studied the elaborate carving of a ten-headed dragon on the dagger's handle.

"Your time has come; release me from this body. Here, through the heart," Black Elder said, wrapping his hands around Helghul's and placing the tip of the blade against a tender spot below his sternum. It was a vulnerable avenue to his heart, without bone to impede the progress of the dagger.

The Elder was pushing hard enough so that the top layer of his clothing was pierced. Helghul stared at the blade in horror, shaking his head and trying to pull back as a circle of blood soaked through the clothing at the pressure point.

Black Elder held firmly to Helghul's hands, preventing him from withdrawing. He could feel the Elder's warm breath on his face. He was certain that the Elder must feel the painful pinch of the blade, though his face did not show it.

You must not shrink from the task before you. My death begins your new life. It will catapult you into a reign that you cannot yet imagine. You have the potential to become the most powerful leader this world has ever known. I have no fear of death; life is eternal. You have my permission, Black Elder said telepathically, still holding firm. *Release me from this body.*

"You do it," Helghul said, wishing the Elder would free his hands or finish the job and plunge the knife deeper.

It doesn't work that way. It is our combined intention that creates this opportunity, Black Elder replied, suddenly becoming contemplative and adding aloud, "Maybe you're not the one I've been waiting for. Perhaps another will come along."

Is he talking about Marcus? Helghul wondered.

Marcus, Black Elder repeated.

He can't outdo me!

Then prove it! You have the opportunity to be remembered, to be monumental in the evolution of consciousness!

A quest for power had always driven Helghul toward his goals. Could it be his destiny to become Black Elder? He knew the Age was descending, that the shift in power meant the rise of a new leader.

Will Marcus become Black Elder if I do not? Helghul wondered. His turmoil abated, and his mind cleared. This was the opportunity he had been waiting for; a puzzle piece had slipped into place.

Black Elder tightened his grip on the knife and caused the handle to dig into the soft skin of the boy's fingers.

This flesh imprisons me. Free me and become the leader you are meant to be!

It was just an instant, an impulsive decision that would affect his lives for millennia. Helghul closed his eyes and turned his face away as he leaned forward and pushed the knife up under the man's sternum, deep into his chest, through the heart of Black Elder.

With a jolt, the atlantium bracelets at Helghul's ankles sparked. The boy felt a powerful rush and was overcome by grandiose feelings of self-importance and confidence as an enormous sigh escaped Black Elder.

The Elder's face softened, and tears welled in his eyes as he felt empathy for the first time in nearly twenty-six thousand years.

"At the time of Atitala's reckoning, you will be called upon . . . a final ceremony will mark the beginning of your reign," Black Elder said in a raspy voice, his tears glowing in the dim light.

Is he crying? Helghul wondered indifferently, as the man slumped to the floor at his feet.

Helghul let him fall, feeling energized. The shadowy shine around the Elder lifted from the corpse. It resembled the man he had been, in a flowing dark cloak, though Helghul couldn't see him.

Take the dagger with you. It will be required for the final ceremony, the voice said inside his head. Helghul pulled the blood-soaked blade from Black Elder, and as the body dropped, his emancipated soul dispersed into the ether.

Helghul cleaned the blade on the dead Elder's robe before stowing it beneath his own. The boy felt nothing at having taken a life. As promised, his empathy was gone.

Helghul stepped over the corpse and wondered how long he would have to wait for the reckoning of Atitala to come.

Marcus and Theron listened intently before climbing from their crates. The heat in the caverns was uncomfortable as the duo maneuvered inelegantly. They secured a variety of atlantium brooches and bracelets to their lower legs to make movement possible in the antigravity environment, and they set out searching with a spring in their step.

They continued to call telepathically for Helghul, but there was no reply.

They began to explore, bouncing lightly along the corridors on the outskirts of Inner Earth into the myriad of caves.

"They all look the same," Theron said, concerned that they were wandering in circles.

"Where's the metropolis of Inner Earth? Where are the Arya?" asked Marcus.

"We must be getting closer," Theron said, feigning confidence.

"Are we naive to think we can save Atitala when the Elders cannot?"

"Cannot or will not? That is the question. I'm not sure I ever really believed we could change what is to come, Marcus," Theron admitted. "But we must try!"

"At least the probability is increased by our efforts even if the outcome is not ours to decide," Marcus said.

Theron looked at her friend. He was a full head shorter than she was, and his thin frame made him appear younger, but his brown eyes were earnest, and his expression was strong and determined.

"You're right, Marcus. There is hope. Let's find Helghul. Maybe he's had more success."

Helghul! Theron called out telepathically as they resumed walking. She scanned for him, closing her eyes to find his mind pictures more easily, but there was no response.

"Listen!"

In the distance there was a faint inconsistent ringing of a bell.

The Guardians! the pair realized with a surge of panic. They headed deeper into the honeycomb tunnels that split in every direction, but they couldn't run as they would have in Outer

Earth; instead, they bounded in large, arching leaps, compelling the atlantium to move them forward.

Glancing back nervously, they attempted to move away from the sounding bell. Marcus noticed there was less atlantium in the caves they were passing, and the area was becoming more desolate and remote.

R-RING, R-RING, R-R-RING . . .

The bell was becoming louder and more consistent. Marcus and Theron stopped their forward momentum and strained to place the direction of the warning, not knowing which way to proceed.

A deep, resonating growl echoed off the walls. The alarm clanged in violent, jerking thrusts.

It's coming from everywhere! I can't tell which way! Theron sent in frantic mind pictures. Marcus held on to her, trying to discern direction. Like Helghul, they were feeling extreme fear for the first time in their lives. In the Golden Age, fear had been contemplated as a state of perception, and was an academic notion to be considered. Here, in this moment, fear was an overwhelming physical, emotional, and mental actuality.

A second roar resonated, filling the tunnels, and completely overpowering the bell. Theron clung to Marcus, and every hair on their bodies prickled at attention as it reverberated through the corridors around them. Judging by how loud it had become, the Guardian was close, but the sounds echoing through the tafoni walls made it impossible to pinpoint the source.

This way! Marcus guessed, and they moved forward out of a wide cavern into one of the many tunnels connecting to it.

Click, click, click. Hooked nails that hung over enormous padded paws clattered against the stone floor with every ring.

In the distance, the Guardian rounded the corridor, filling the entire height and width of the tunnel's opening. The pair screamed involuntarily, and Marcus protectively stepped in front of Theron, though she was bigger and stronger than he was.

They stared at the ferocious lionlike creature, momentarily transfixed. A curly mane and bulky metal yoke covered its muscular barrel chest, and its batlike ears twitched. The majestic Guardian growled, baring its teeth, and the atlantium studs on its collar glowed. Even from afar, they could see the strength rippling through its jaws and forepaws. Its protuberant eyes were dense and without emotion as it appraised Marcus and Theron mercilessly. Its nostrils flared and quivered while its black tongue licked its jagged fangs, tasting the air, tasting their scent, and jerking its broad nose. *RING, RING,* warned the bell, as the Guardian leapt forward.

"Go! Get back to the open cavern!" Marcus shouted, sending Theron ahead of him.

It could devour a Nephilim in two bites, he thought frantically as they propelled forward.

The predator roared as it gave chase, and their bones shook. They could hear its guttural chuffing and armor clanking with every movement. With their arms pumping, legs pumping, hearts pumping, they leapt forward. The Guardian drew closer, and Marcus lagged behind Theron.

Marcus looked back, and the pursuer glared at him, bearing down on them with its bushy black head and gnashing teeth. He could feel the heat of the enormous beast, but worse was the resonant promise of suffering. Theron turned and saw her image reflected in Marcus's eyes. She knew he had intentionally placed himself between her and the Guardian to give her more time, to let her get away. It had all happened so quickly. They had entered a high, open cavern, but the hunter was nearly upon them.

"Will yourself to the ceiling!" Marcus shouted, and Theron obeyed.

Marcus pushed Theron's feet upward, thrusting her faster, out of the reach of the Guardian. The snarling monster was nearly on Marcus. The boy mentally commanded the atlantium to lift him, and an unstable burst of energy pitched him forward. He used frantic swimming motions to propel himself faster.

The creature charged. Marcus saw it leap as he pushed up and off the cave wall. The animal narrowly missed him and collided with the stone. It fell back onto the floor, shaking its massive head.

With a disgruntled snort, it splattered the lower walls with gobs of foamy drool.

Marcus and Theron looked down on the Guardian as it circled angrily below, staring up at them and evaluating its next move. A second Guardian entered the cavern, snarling and ringing as it came. They were pressed against the hot ceiling—safe . . . but not for long.

To their horror, the Guardian began the vertical climb up the wall toward them. This unfortunate development proved that the creature had the ability to commandeer the atlantium at its throat. Marcus had hoped its crystal adorned collar had been merely ornamental. There was no escape as it stalked them, perpendicular to the floor. Its head was inverted, looking back over its shoulder at them. Marcus and Theron grabbed on to one another, bracing for impact.

RING, RING, warned the bell—too late. The first Guardian leapt and cut the distance between them.

Suddenly, a streak of light blinded them, and they felt a lurch.

"Shall we move on?" Willowy Man asked softly. Marcus and Theron opened their eyes to a changed scene. A gap had opened in the rock, and they had been pulled through. Wrapped in the Tunnel-Keeper's long arms, they were now traveling through a twisting channel. They hugged him and each other while tears of relief dripped from their faces. Though they were safely out of reach of the Guardian, they panted, and their blood was pulsing with adrenaline.

"Thank you!" Theron gasped, and the rescuer nodded respectfully. They were so close that they could see Willowy Man's kind eyes, which were the same pale pink as his lips.

"Thank you!" Marcus echoed. "How did you know? How did you find us?"

"You were never lost. I have been aware of your presence since you first hid yourselves in the atlantium," Willowy Man replied with a mischievous glint in his eye.

"You sent the Guardian to scare us?" Marcus asked in disbelief.

"Great Jupiter, no! How cruel that would be. When it appeared you needed my assistance, I stepped in."

Marcus and Theron felt Willowy Man gracefully steer them along the fire lines. It was a dance of undulating currents, balance, light, and color.

"Marcus, you were so brave and clever," Theron said into the hair on the top of his head, and she saw him in a way she never had before.

"I'm not brave."

Theron had always admired Marcus's intellect and kindness, but she had not recognized his courage. Her thoughts turned to Helghul.

"Willowy Man," Theron began urgently, concerned for her missing friend. "Oh, is that . . . I don't know what we should call you," she stammered, though the warmth and kindness that emanated from the Old One was intended to put her at ease.

"I have had many names. I am not particularly attached to any of them."

"We have to find our friend Helghul before the Guardians do," Theron explained.

"There are worse things in the tunnels than the Guardians. Your friend is in no physical danger. We are going to him now. I suspect you did not tell White Elder that you have come?" Willowy Man guessed.

"We did not," Theron admitted.

"It is not her journey," Willowy Man said thoughtfully. "Perhaps you will tell *me* why you have come?" he said, and Marcus and Theron eagerly explained their objective: to convince the Inner Earthlings to save Atitala and to transfer her inhabitants inward.

"Can you help us?" Marcus asked.

"Yours is a noble but naive objective. Inner Earth dwellers do not welcome human guests, and Inner Earth is not habitable for the human race long term due to poor oxygen and extreme temperatures. Arya are of a higher frequency, and your two cultures are incompatible."

"What about your Lemurian home—Shambhala?" Theron asked hopefully.

"No amount of sneaking or searching will reveal Shambhala; one must be invited to enter that sacred place. But even more, you must consider that the conscious people of Atitala cannot abandon Outer Earth as she enters a time of trial. The descent into the Darker Ages is not a punishment; it is rather a schoolroom where potentials and possibilities are born out. It is where souls incarnate to evolve consciousness until the cycles are no longer necessary."

"So there is nothing to be done?" Marcus asked dejectedly.

"There is much to be done by brave ones such as you! There must be light in these coming Ages," Willowy Man said. "But the laws and nature of the universe cannot be superseded. We must be quick; the fire lines are traveling toward Atitala now, and your time here has already taken a toll."

"What kind of toll?" Marcus asked.

"You will see. Better you just see," Willowy Man replied.

☨ ☨ ☨

Helghul was crouched behind one of the countless flying machines being stored in an expansive cavern that appeared to be a landing strip. It was a treasure trove of resources that would remain hidden to the Outer World in the coming Ages. The heat was unbearable, and beads of sweat dripped from his brow. He was aware of his heavy breathing and dire thirst, and he was anxious to return to Atitala. Thanks to his recent interaction with Black Elder, his confidence was high, and he knew he could commandeer one of the disc-shaped vimana using the atlantium at his ankles. The steep tunnels must lead to Outer Earth. He would fly out and find his way home to Atitala—a hero—without the aid of Willowy Man.

There were several Arya on the far side of the massive room, but, like the rest of the Inner Earth Dwellers whom Helghul had avoided, they showed no sign of perceiving his presence.

He remained hidden, plotting his escape, with no intention of approaching the illuminated beings.

Helghul's original motive for entering Inner Earth had been replaced by thoughts of boundless ambition. He had no selfless concern for the people of Atitala or their suffering.

He wondered if he would be received as an Elder upon his return home, or if it would be his secret to endure until it was finalized. He protectively stroked the dagger tucked into the waist-band beneath his tunic. The lumpy carved knobs of the dragon heads poked and bruised his hip.

Helghul wondered whom he could confide in. Who would believe him? Marcus? Theron? His parents? Could he tell them? Should he? Frankly, he realized, he no longer cared what they thought.

Helghul did not notice that the Arya had seen him and were now gliding, silently closer. He was oblivious, consumed by his ambition and staring at the flying discs. Had his thoughts remained pure and selfless, the Arya might not have perceived him, but as Helghul's thoughts spiraled, becoming selfish and dark, his energy had assaulted their senses.

The Arya were only a few paces away in his periphery when, without warning, there was a luminescent flash. Helghul was scooped up by Willowy Man just as Marcus and Theron had been, but he reacted with far less gratitude. For a moment Helghul thought it was his own powers, some part of having become Black Elder. He was disappointed to find he had been pulled into the current by the Tunnel-Keeper and was hurling toward Atitala, reunited with his friends.

Theron was filled with relief and welcomed Helghul with a hug, burying her face in his neck. "I'm so glad we found you. When we saw the Guardians . . . you were gone . . . I thought . . . ," Theron said. Her voice broke as she clung to him.

Helghul felt the softness of her arms and skin. He was flooded with love and desire. Theron was the kindest and brightest girl he had ever known. He had always assumed that someday they would couple. She would be his, and together they would rule the Ages to come.

Marcus watched his best friends, relieved that Helghul had returned safely, but for the first time he felt a tinge of envy. He turned away, ashamed of his selfish thoughts. He blamed himself, unaware that this emotion was yet another sign that the decline of the Golden Age had begun. Marcus hardly had time to greet Helghul before they landed with a mild thump, coming to a stop.

"The Elders await your return," Willowy Man announced as he expertly circled his hands and opened the portal before them.

It was sunrise, and dim pink-and-orange beams lit the horizon, highlighting the early-morning mist and waking the chirping jungle below. The trio stepped out of the stone wall beside the quarry entrance. The Elders stood waiting, with the Nephilim in an orderly semicircle behind them.

Helghul discarded the atlantium he had been using to weigh himself down and stepped out of the cave's arched opening. With a smooth wave of his arms, the Tunnel-Keeper closed the portal and was gone.

Helghul emerged cautiously, his gaze flitting from face to face, gauging the Elders. The intuitive acumen of the Elders was so strong that he didn't dare look them directly in the eyes. Marcus and Theron followed him nervously, holding hands.

Do they know? Helghul wondered.

The Elders greeted them with gentle reproach and relief, followed by a barrage of questions about their experiences in Inner Earth. Theron and Marcus willingly recounted the story of their dramatic rescue from the Guardian and their failed hopes to relocate their fellow Atitalans. Helghul revealed little and remained silent about his encounter with Black Elder. He was *too* quiet; it wasn't typical, and Marcus looked at him suspiciously.

"What happened to you in there?" Marcus whispered, sensing that his friend was keeping a secret.

"Nothing," Helghul flatly lied, but his eyes were missing the spark that Marcus knew so well.

"Why are you so quiet?"

"Just disappointed that we failed," Helghul lied again. He had never lied in the past, but for the first time in his life, it seemed necessary. The difference was that he now felt no obligation to the listener. It was in his best interest to lie, and nothing else mattered.

Deep down, Helghul wanted to tell Marcus that he had become an Elder. He wanted to describe Black Elder and to share how powerful he felt. But he didn't want to tell *this* Marcus. This Marcus who had placed himself between Theron and the Guardian making himself some sort of hero. *This* Marcus who had held Theron's hand as they walked to meet the Elders. This Marcus would not be impressed by him. *This* Marcus was a threat.

He just needs some time, Marcus thought. But he was wrong. Helghul had changed. They all had.

Over the months and years following their visit to Inner Earth, life changed considerably. Helghul and Marcus grew farther apart every day. Despite Marcus's best efforts, Helghul had become aloof and distant. He had grown increasingly competitive, and eventually Marcus moved out of Helghul's parents' home and took a small single dwelling next to Bapoo's.

As much as she tried, Theron could not ignore the change in Helghul. He was unable to mute the prideful conceit that radiated from him. His experience in Inner Earth had taken a toll.

Chapter 3

First Love

Atitala, five years later

Theron stood on the terrace of the Grand Palace. It was an architectural and artistic masterpiece at the center of Atitala, with countless rooms and windows that had been carved over centuries into the natural rock of the mountain. The central balcony featured a colossal golden statue of four horses pulling a human in a chariot. It was not the representation of an idol or god, but was a symbol of the divine in every person. The horses represented the four elements—air, water, fire, and earth—that made up the material universe. The chariot represented the material body, the vehicle that the soul inhabited, and the androgynous human form within the chariot represented the fifth element—ether or soul. Beneath the chariot flowed a sparkling waterfall that dropped through the center of the horse hooves into a clear pool far below.

The water represented transformation, a return to the waters and to the death–rebirth cycle.

Theron was now in her eighteenth year, and she radiated strength and confidence. Her body had grown fuller and her face more angular. She had a prominent nose that was oddly striking. Her narrow green eyes squinted almost closed when she laughed, and days spent on the sunny coast had left her fair skin freckled.

She scanned the two steep natural-stone carved stairways that flanked the waterfall and led from the palace to the multicolored marketplace tents below. Her white robe and flowing chestnut hair blew in the gentle breeze as she searched the landscape through rainbow prisms that were reflected in the sunlight.

The city was laid out in concentric circles, with alternating channels of water and land connected by living root, vine, and stone bridges. At the center was the palace, the Grand Hall, the Senate chamber, the marketplace, and the common areas. Next, were the dwellings, and on the outer edges were the farmlands. All of the man-made adaptations blended seamlessly with the natural surroundings. The white, black, and red stone buildings were topped with sturdy glass atriums, and beyond the fields to the west stood a white limestone pyramid with a gold capstone.

It was the eve of the Summer Solstice Festival, and Theron had agreed to slip away briefly. The past few weeks had been unusually demanding, but Theron had remained hardworking and dutiful. Marcus had planned a surprise, and she was looking forward to spending some time with him.

"Have the sacred crystals been laid out in the Grand Hall?" Marcus asked from behind, startling her as he landed a vimana glider on the balcony.

"Where did you get the atlantium for a glider?" Theron asked.

"White Elder said you need some time in nature, and I was happy to oblige."

"She wouldn't do that, Marcus," Theron replied. Life without atlantium was more physically demanding, though the Elders still had access to a limited amount to assist in larger jobs. But it was no longer readily available and was rarely used.

"She gave it to me to complete my work on the White Pyramid, and I finished early," Marcus said as he pulled Theron into his arms.

Marcus had changed drastically over the past five years. Where the boy had been skinny and childlike, he was now a full head taller than Theron. His shoulders had become wide and muscular, and his face was handsome and chiseled, topped by a crown of wavy black hair. In contrast to Theron's fair complexion, Marcus's skin was brown, and looked as though he had been buttered and baked for a feast. The humility and loving nature that had endeared him to everyone as a child still radiated around him.

Marcus stroked Theron's cheek, removing a long strand of hair that had blown across her mouth, and kissed her.

"I've missed you," he murmured as they hugged.

"Marcus, you're beautiful," Theron said with a kiss.

"So are you," he replied, taking Theron's other hand as they stared into each other's eyes. She could still see the clever, courageous boy who had placed himself between her and the Guardian, the boy who had always been gentle and steady. The shine surrounding Marcus and Theron had united them, and they basked in each other, unwilling to move.

It had been five cycles around the sun since their adventure to Inner Earth, five years of growing closer—rife with months and years of confusion and discord as they struggled to understand Helghul's strange transformation.

Their friend had become distant and self-centered. They had been determined to maintain, and then repair, the fading friendship, but every time they tried, he acted selfishly and further alienated them.

Together, Marcus and Theron mourned the loss of a dear friend, while at the same time their budding romance intensified. They were inseparable, and their estrangement from Helghul only gave them more in common.

"Come fly with me. There's no reason to give it back quite yet. You know you want to!" Marcus said, pulling her toward the vimana.

"We can't."

"We can," he said, wrapping a quick arm around her and smoothly nudging her onto the vimana in front of him. She allowed herself to be drawn in. Before she could change her mind, Marcus channeled his intentions into the atlantium crystal, enabling the transport to lift off the terrace. Their stomachs lurched as they plunged through the mist of the falls, and cool spray covered them.

"Everyone will see us, Marcus!" Theron said, but it was too late. They were sailing on the air, and though Theron knew White Elder would disapprove, her daring nature longed for an adventure.

Theron had always loved flying. It was the convenience she had missed the most. Except for the birds, the skies around Atitala were quiet since the Willowy Man had collected and removed all of the atlantium. Machinists had been searching ancient archives for other options and had found a few that did not require fossil fuels, but they were slow and archaic compared to the ease of the gliders and vimana.

Marcus steered the glider easily, and Theron's flowing hair blew wildly as they rode.

"Where are you taking me?" she asked.

"You'll see," he replied.

Theron leaned back against his strong torso as they playfully dipped and weaved through the trees. It was exhilarating to fly again, to feel the freedom and to be one with the air around them.

As they passed, the Elders appeared below them in an expansive field of rich black soil. Theron buried her head in Marcus's shoulder guiltily—they'd been discovered! The Senate often convened outdoors, walking while in discussion, but today was profoundly important. She should have remembered. The first crop of the season had been harvested, and as was the tradition, they were honoring the sowing of the new seeds. White Elder was surrounded by a large congregation of farmers and their families. The harvests had been dwindling in recent years, and the Elders were concerned for the food supply.

Green Elder led the ceremony as the teacher of heart and earthly sciences. She communed with the Elementals, which were the primary parts of all matter. She held the seeds in her hands, and the others followed her, whispering their intentions and blessings into the seeds. They filled each with gratitude for the abundance and the miraculous seedlings that would grow to nourish and heal their nation. They walked barefoot through the soil, honoring the needs and connection between the humans, plants, and the planet.

White Elder looked up disapprovingly as Marcus and Theron passed overhead.

"It is good that they enjoy their youth and freedom," Orange Elder said. She was Atitala's master of personal, social, and sexual human energies.

"Let them enjoy this time; it will end soon enough," Red Elder added in a gruff voice.

"Yes, they have been working hard. Everything for the solstice ceremony has been prepared," Yellow Elder said, placing a comforting hand on White Elder's shoulder as Marcus and Theron disappeared in the distance.

"Can we truly be prepared?" White Elder asked with a sigh. Their hearts had been heavy for some time, knowing that they could not.

><><><><><><

"I never tire of the beauty here. Look," Marcus said, pointing at hundreds of colorful orphan birds that resembled a cross between a peacock and a crane except for their beaks and talons, which more resembled those of an eagle. The birds nested and floated near the beach below. Marcus's voice mingled with the wind as they swooped through the jungle canopy and brushed the tops of the high palms at their feet.

"I can feel that you're troubled. Will White Elder be so terribly angry?" Marcus asked.

"No. It's not that. She's been unusually grim," Theron replied, comforted by his closeness. Marcus had felt it too. It was not only White Elder who was uneasy. They knew change was upon them, and the uncertainty of it was unsettling.

"Let's enjoy this while we can," Marcus said, gesturing to the paradise around them. "Who knows what we will have to face . . . or when." He tightened his grip around her waist. The couple were silent as they flew on.

Marcus and Theron arrived at the inland lake at the base of the quarry. Theron stood, her arms open wide and face turned to the sun, and took a deep, cleansing breath. It was the same lake that the Nephilim had dropped into the day of the balloon diversion. Their adventure to Inner Earth seemed so long ago. The lake was surrounded by rocky cliffs to the north and dense jungle to the south. The young couple had the remote water hole to themselves, except for the pink dolphins that acknowledged them by cascading bubbles under them. The duo swam beneath the surface of the clear pool, just below the steep cliffs adjacent to the atlantium quarry, communicating in detailed mind pictures.

I am so grateful for this. Thank you, she said blissfully.

I am so grateful for you, Marcus replied. The couple surfaced together with a splash. Treading water, their cool lips connected. It was warm and exciting, and they were filled with the most wonderful feeling as Marcus's hands found the curve of her nude hips. There was nothing but skin and water between them.

In the Golden Age, sex did not dominate the human psyche; it was for pleasure and procreation but had only positive aspects of sharing each other in material form. Marcus and Theron were virgins. Though they understood that intercourse was said to be immensely pleasurable, they also knew that it did not compare to coupling within the Universal Grid. When a couple joined in the grid, they became entangled as soulmates.

The Universal Grid was the absolute self-existing matrix that contained all life and connected all energy and matter in the universe. It was an infinite field of consciousness. The grid was a web that was observable once material limitations were shed—when a soul wasn't limited to the body and could then navigate the highway of light.

In Atitala, couples valued a higher joining, an intense union that could only be achieved once one was able to astral-travel. Astral-traveling was the ability to leave one's physical body and journey as a light being, faster than the speed of thought. When beings bonded with one another in the grid, they permanently entangled their subatomic particles and evolved as soulmates. It was the choice to link future incarnations. It was not a guarantee of infinite bliss; it was a meaningful, energetic contract to remain connected and evolve together even though there could be lifetimes where their paths might not cross. To take a soulmate was to commit to a partnership of helping each soul grow and expand into the best version of itself.

"Marcus, will you choose to couple with me?" Theron asked. Her words were slow and deliberate. It was typical in their society for the women to proffer this option.

"You would choose me as your soulmate?" Marcus said, his voice catching in his throat.

"No other," she whispered, kissing him again. "We would meet again in lifetimes to come."

"I have loved you since we were children . . . I once thought you and Helghul might be destined for more."

"It's you. It has always been you," Theron said, kissing him again.

A loud cracking interrupted their reverie, and suddenly an enormous boulder splashed down dangerously close to them.

"Move!" Marcus shouted as the water surged, nearly smashing them against the rocks. Struggling, they looked up to see another boulder chased by many smaller rocks speeding toward them. The swimmers dove but were unable to evade the debris raining down on them. They pushed through the resistant water while stones painfully pummeled them. Like a freight train, a large rock barreled through the water, ramming into Theron, ripping her from Marcus's side. He watched helplessly as she was forced away from him and driven deeper. Marcus, still under siege from the falling rocks, grabbed hold of a heavy sinking stone as it hurled past, pursuing her to the lake bottom, where she was trapped.

Theron was in excruciating pain as they struggled, pushing and tugging against the boulder that had ensnared her right leg. Their panicked thoughts intermingled, though they tried to remain focused.

It's not moving! Burning, burning, she thought as her lungs pleaded for release.

I'll get it, I'll shift it! Marcus projected as Theron struggled frantically against the stubborn mass. She watched in astonishment, her eyes wild with alarm as Marcus suddenly swam away. *Don't leave me!* she projected, just an instant before her straining mouth burst like a balloon, and her body began to fill with water. Marcus felt the words and thoughts jumbled in her telepathic chaos as the bubbles of her last breath followed him to the surface.

I'm not leaving! It's our only chance, he thought, but there was no response. Theron's telepathic communication had ceased.

She's dying! Dying! Marcus thought as he exploded through the surface gasping, his own lungs burning. The atlantium crystal on the vimana glider was his only hope.

The rockslide had opened a small gap in the cliff, and the air was thick with dust. The desperate young man heaved himself out of the water, his feet slipping as he lunged up the rock. His body was being pushed to its limits as he hurried to retrieve the crystal.

Move! Faster! I have to go faster! It's taking too long!

Through the opening in the cliff where the boulders had once been, the gourd-headed Nephilim and several others watched the frenzied man indifferently, though they had triggered the avalanche by carelessly tossing a boulder aside.

Got it! I'm too late! Rise boulder, Rise! Marcus projected, diving back into the pool and summoning the power to activate the crystal. Marcus touched the trembling boulder with the atlantium, and it responded to his mental command, lifting from his motionless love. Marcus pulled Theron from the water, ignoring the jagged rocks on the shore that scraped and bruised them.

No, Theron! Don't go! Come back to me! he screamed telepathically as he breathed for her—in, out, two, three. *Breathe!* Her torso
rose and fell with his air. He pumped her chest, compelling her
heart. His heart! His blood was pounding, painful and frantic at
the absurdity of this unlikely accident.

Don't leave me! he pleaded.

Finally, she sputtered; there was a freshwater flood and coughing, and Marcus turned her on her side. She was alive! Marcus was
overwhelmed, and tears of gratitude replaced his tears of horror.

Theron lay limp in Marcus's arms, her breathing ragged.

"I thought you left me," she sputtered, opening her eyes and
gasping. She remembered the helplessness she had felt as she had
watched him swim away.

"I will never leave you," he promised, cradling her and show-
ing her the atlantium in his hand. His voice was muffled as he
placed his lips to her head.

Their wet skin was speckled with sticking sand. Marcus's chest
heaved as he stroked her dripping hair. She was all length and
limbs, and her crushed leg was bloody and bent at an awkward
angle. Marcus held her as still as possible to reduce her pain. He
shuddered at the realization that he had almost lost her.

Helghul lurked above, glowering down at them, his belly
churning with envy and disappointment. From above the glimmering lake, the unsettled dust particles made it difficult to see.
He had watched the couple's misfortune, callously pondering the
missed opportunity. He had been there all along, hidden, observing their ordeal with selfish interest. The man's muscular jaw
flexed as his thoughts vacillated between extremes.

Since his meeting with Black Elder, Helghul had functioned
in a state of cold and calculating clarity. His love for Theron
had turned possessive and self-centered, and she had immediately noticed the change in him and had resisted his advances,
pulling away.

Though they had been young and uncommitted prior to
entering Inner Earth, Helghul had always assumed that someday they would be together. Throughout the years after their

return, Helghul took no responsibility for her perceived change of heart, choosing instead to see her and Marcus's pairing as a massive betrayal.

Helghul hoped that Theron would survive the accident and choose him. Together, they would create a mighty empire. However, he had alternately hoped that she would drown so he would not have to endure seeing her couple with Marcus. He had been at odds with what he had desired for Theron, but he had no divergent thoughts regarding Marcus. Helghul had certainly wished his former best friend dead.

I'll never leave you, Helghul had overheard, and his hatred burned. Theron had asked Marcus to couple with her in the grid. *Outrageous!*

It is *my* destiny, *my* right! he thought. Helghul believed to his core that she belonged with *him*, not Marcus.

Helghul made his way back through the caverns toward the far eastern exit. He didn't want to be seen near the site of the accident. As he walked, he wondered what fault would have been his, what blame . . . if Theron had died. He wondered how he would be judged in tribunal, the counsel between incarnations where one's choices and deeds were weighed to determine the lessons and lives to come. He shrank from the potential consequences of his inaction, but his conscience remained unmoved.

Helghul continued to contemplate how he had watched Theron drowning without empathy. He had thought only of his own needs and how she could help him in the future. He was convinced that she was the best logical partner for him: smart, attractive, well born. He could not deny that he still preferred her to all others. He loved her, and he was fascinated by the sinister feelings that had come over him so readily. The realization that he would rather kill her than lose her was startling. He was aware that dark emotions had begun to fill him more often, but rather than being concerned, he felt mostly intrigued. Atitala was changing.

Theron's sputtering and coughing finally subsided. Marcus wrapped her bloody leg with a strip of his clothing and placed her carefully in his lap for transport. He held the shard of atlantium crystal in his palm, returning it to his gliders console, and then reactivated his energy for the return home. He had alerted the healers, who met them at the home of White Elder. Theron was given relief from her pain, and Marcus was sent away while she was being treated. Despite his desire to remain with Theron, Marcus was given no choice but to leave.

Throughout Atitala, people were preparing for the festivities that would take place the following day. Solstice was a celebration of light that was anticipated by all. This summer solstice was especially important because on the morning of the celebration, the Sirius Star, which was the brightest in the sky and could be seen from anywhere on Earth, would reemerge from behind the sun. It was called the Star of Death and Rebirth.

The entire unitary had painstakingly prepared for the event, which would be attended by the Elders, guests from outlying lands, and all of Atitala's citizens.

Later that afternoon, Theron woke. Her leg had been reconstructed from the knee down, and there was hardly a mark, thanks to advancements in the regeneration process. In the Golden Age, there were few illnesses that could not be eradicated, and developments with healing vibration were at their peak. In addition to these healing advances, the Earth's energies were harnessed through the White Pyramid and created an electromagnetic field that prevented the breakdown of the body and mind by neutralizing the impact of free radicals. This allowed people to enjoy great longevity, without the threat of illness. It was normal for healthy Atitalans to live hundreds of years if they avoided accidents.

Theron marveled at how close she had come to dying as White Elder stood beside her, concern deepening the lines in her face. Theron smiled, feeling clear and rested.

How did this happen? White Elder thought protectively, sending her question telepathically to her daughter. The woman stroked her child's forehead, and Theron enjoyed the tender moment.

It was an accident, Theron said.

There are no accidents. Your injury comes at a most unfortunate time, White Elder answered, dropping her hands to her side.

I can fulfill my duties for summer solstice, not to worry.

You're aware there is much more afoot these days than solstice, daughter. "Heal well. I am glad you are safe. I must leave you," the leader said aloud, exiting with a directed nod to the healer in the corner. Theron wished she would stay, longing for signs that she held a special place in her mother's heart. The affection of White Elder was so unconditional toward everything and everyone that Theron secretly wished for more. She desired her mother's approval, above all, and she was grateful her mother hadn't chastised her for using the glider.

When Marcus arrived at his quarters, he was greeted by Bapoo. He, unlike Marcus, had remained small and skinny and looked more like Marcus's little brother than his contemporary. His hazel eyes sparkled with amusement. Bapoo was witty and had always been sincere and loyal. Marcus was grateful for his friendship.

"I hear you almost killed the future White Elder?" Bapoo said.

"Ugh! I feel badly enough," Marcus replied.

"I'm glad she's all right," Bapoo said, growing serious. "Another young one has gone missing." Marcus shook his head in confusion. It was the second child to disappear in as many days.

"Where can they be? Certainly no harm has come to them," Marcus said hopefully. It was unfathomable.

The Elders were aware of the growing endarkenment of their citizens. There was a gradual metamorphosis occurring, and they worked tirelessly to guide and teach their people. It was a descending turn, and the Elders prepared for what would come.

Crime was a new phenomenon, a throwback to ages long ago. Citizens had begun to covet, and to compete with one another. Envy was becoming widespread, and an insipid selfishness and discontent percolated behind closed doors.

⋈ ⋈ ⋈

When the Summer Solstice Festival began at sunrise the next morning, Marcus was at the right hand of Theron. It had been a busy and inspiring day, and now they were gathered to honor the sunset. White Elder gave the signal, and the tranquil harp music abruptly ended and was replaced by a blast of horns heralding the commencement of the ceremony.

The leader watched from her central vantage point at the southern end of the room. Her uneasiness was apparent to no one but Theron, who felt it like an oyster feels a grain of sand against its soft underbelly. The other Elders sat next to White Elder in a semicircle: Yellow, Grey, Red, Orange, Green, and Blue. The visitors took places of honor around the majestic Grand Hall, magnificent in their multicolored robes, saris, and jewels.

The white-robed citizens of Atitala filled the remainder of the vast space, each of them highlighted by distinct auras that glowingly displayed their individual shines. The gorgeous white, black, and red marble amphitheater held hundreds of thousands of people easily, with balconies and tunnels throughout to prevent congestion. The space was ingeniously designed for optimal viewing and auditory projection.

Huge gold pillars encircled the center court, supporting an intricate glass ceiling that was at least five hundred feet from end to end. The design allowed light from the dazzling sun and moon to illuminate the chamber throughout the seasons.

As the burst of jubilant horns sounded, the citizens took their seats and became quiet in anticipation. The demonstrators and performers were seated in rows on the opposite side of the vast auditorium.

Across the hall, Helghul stared bitterly at Theron's chosen mate. His rival was undeniably handsome and intelligent but lacked Helghul's ambition and drive. Marcus was patient and easygoing, while Helghul was intense and competitive. Marcus did not seek notoriety, nor had he set his sights on the Senate despite his obvious popularity and ability. Helghul concluded that Marcus was beneath him, but it did nothing to ease his envy.

The festival proceeded with singing, performances by the children and special guests, and a recitation of the words written on the Emerald Tablet by Red Elder.

Once the sun had set on the longest day of the year and the silver moonlight shone in from the center of the glass ceiling, it was time for everyone's favorite part of the celebration.

"Please prepare for the Merging," Grey Elder called out from his place next to White Elder, cuing the audience to merge with one another. Merging was when the people intentionally joined their energy in a display of oneness. Through a chorus of deliberate octaves and conscious notes, the room was electrified, and buzzed with mounting cosmic energy. People stood, holding hands or linking their arms together.

"Aum, Aum, Aum," they chanted. The Grand Hall was abuzz as a ball of light began to form in the center of the room. The entire congregation sang as the light ball divided, first in half and then again, until it resembled an eight-cell embryo cluster. The light projected an imprint of the egg onto the white marble floor, and the resulting two-dimensional symbol was the seed of life. The room burst into a kaleidoscope of color and forms, creating a dramatic laser light show.

"Merge," White Elder called out, and the seed of life on the floor expanded into the flower of life, doubling and redoubling its boundaries, forming a 3-D web over them. The many lights and shapes around the room connected in a dome above the people, with continual, evolving patterns.

The geometric forms moved and expanded, reaching up to the glass ceiling, ready to breach its confines. Marcus and Theron stood face-to-face, their hands tightly clasped and their eyes locked on each other. During the Merging, the illusion of separation disappeared. Joy glowed in their faces. Each individual became a part of the whole; his or her discrete worries, desires, and needs were forgotten. They were reminded that they were all interconnected and inseparable. The display sparked and pulsed.

Suddenly a current of confusion rippled through the connection. Everyone felt the uncertainty and doubt as something went wrong.

Just as the group envisioned expanding their connection beyond the dome into the starry night sky, they faltered. The image flickered, and large sections of the connection faded. There were audible gasps, and a wave of fear—foreign to the Grand Hall—flowed through like an icy flood. All of the voices stopped their hum, and the lights and connection disappeared. The crowd erupted into frantic whispers.

The people of Atitala had never known a time when their wills and voices were not purely united; the sacred Merging ceremony had never wavered, at least not in Atitala. They were shocked, looking to the Elders for an explanation.

"Find peace within you," Yellow Elder said serenely. His wrinkled face and almond-shaped eyes remained calm.

"Those without fear are free," Green Elder said. Her large brown eyes sought to reassure her people, and she opened her arms in a soothing gesture.

"Remember our oneness and unity," White Elder instructed. "Join now and clear your minds."

A number of visiting dignitaries ignored White Elder's instructions and noisily ushered their families toward the exits. Helghul and a few others had slipped out among them. The remaining crowd joined the Elders in a calming meditation, but many were unable to release their concern. They were anxious to leave the Grand Hall. They wanted to discuss the failed Merging, and they wondered what lay ahead for them. The fear and uncertainty they were feeling reflected a change in their frequencies.

Bapoo made his way across the room to Theron and Marcus, and together the three of them were determined to hold steady under the strange circumstances. They reassured one another silently, clutching arms and trying to shed the anxiety bubbling up in their guts. Their other friends, Yashoda, Kushim, and Holt, joined them.

Outside, Helghul was filled with excitement by what had occurred. Amid the chaos he had felt empowered, as if Black Elder had once again held a hand to his chest, sending waves of dark energy through him. Despite the confusion and concern around him, Helghul had remained composed and was invigorated by the turmoil. He had not been participating in the Merging when it faltered. He had been pretending, going through the outward motions and imagining a time when he would be in power and his talents would be recognized and appreciated. He was excited that the Merging had failed. He had been delighted to witness the weakness of the others. It meant that he was closer to becoming leader over them all.

The Atitalans made their way into the streets, ushering their children home and chattering nervously.

"Did you feel that . . . that . . . *feeling*? What was it?"

"What went wrong?"

"How can it be?"

"The end of an Age? Surely we must have more time?"

"Does anyone know what will happen now?"

The Elders calmed the citizens as best they could, but they offered few answers and were eager to get into the White Pyramid and around the Emerald Tablet. Important duties awaited them.

White Elder requested that her daughter join her and the other Elders in the White Pyramid, and though Marcus was reluctant to have her go, the ever-dutiful Theron departed without hesitation. Marcus did not know that inside the pyramid, Theron would be made privy to the astounding potential of the Emerald Tablet. It was a momentous secret that would eventually lay dormant in her psyche, waiting to be recalled.

Marcus returned to his chamber. All of the others were with their families, and he was left to speculate alone. Marcus contemplated the breakdown of the Merging, and the gravity of the unexpected fail filled him with melancholy and set him to reflecting on the loss of his parents and his best friend.

They hadn't abandoned him—not really—but suddenly, subconsciously, the losses felt like rejection, and he had to remind himself they were not. The descent from the Golden Age brought with it unfamiliar waves of negative emotions and the first stirrings of ego. Marcus resisted and turned his thoughts to Theron—her touch, her laugh, the uncertainty of life ahead—and he dreamed of their future together.

Chapter 4

The Decline of the Golden Age

Following the solstice, there were nights in Atitala when the ground moaned and the sky rumbled. The weather had begun to change. As if conjured, violent winds blew and sudden storms swept over the city without warning. Lightning strikes claimed property and lives, and the thunder boomed.

Despite the care paid to the sowing of the seeds, the yields had been poor, and the harvest was a disappointment. But the most distressing of the recent developments were the continued disappearances. It had begun with one missing child—an infant missing from the cot next to his parents while they slept. There was no evidence, only a window they had innocently left open. Then another, a toddler, gone from the marketplace while her parents shopped nearby. She had dashed lightheartedly ahead, mingling in a sea of legs, and then suddenly she had vanished. The frantic parents searched in confusion; the colorful fruit-and-vegetable carts hid no playful child. Her voice was gone, her mind pictures disappeared all at once, and her parents could not reach her in any manner. It was unheard of, yet it happened again and again. Children continued to disappear without explanation.

Nine young ones, all under four years of age, had inexplicably gone missing. The citizens were hopeful, praying for the safe return of the lost little ones while growing understandably fearful and protective of their own children.

White Elder and her Senate worked tirelessly to solve the mystery of the disappearances, but despite their suspicions and intuition, they were unable to stem the flow or find the children.

In lecture, Yellow Elder informed his pupils of an important development. The diminutive instructor looked around the stone amphitheater at the four thousand faces ranging from early teens to early twenties. The room spiraled like a nautilus shell to the high cathedral ceiling, and his voice carried effortlessly, amplified to every ear.

"I know you have all recognized the changes in Atitala since solstice," he said, walking out from behind his writing table. The tired students had been sitting a long time but were suddenly alert and interested. Yellow Elder stroked his sparse white goatee as he continued, "Our world has clearly entered an age of turmoil. People have become increasingly fearful and suspicious." He paused.

"Creation, destruction, and change have been the cycle since the beginning of time. The world we know will eventually collapse and be lost to chaos. There are those who will eagerly call upon the dark energies to utilize them and make the most of this shift," Yellow Elder explained, and the students stirred anxiously.

"But who?" Kushim asked nervously.

"We don't know who or how many have already been corrupted. The time of the Emissary is near. The Great Cycle requires that the chosen of our people be called." Yellow Elder waited as the students buzzed with excitement and disbelief.

"Who will the Elders choose?" Bapoo asked, his voice echoing through the hall.

"As we speak, the Senate is preparing to choose from among *you*, the students of Atitala," he said to an uproar. He raised his calming hands, and the students hushed. "Not all of you are destined to become Emissaries. Many hopefuls will be eliminated."

"How?" Marcus called out. Yellow Elder scanned the crowd for the source of the voice.

"By your ineptitude," Helghul interjected loudly, and a small chuckle erupted from some of his fellow classmates. Marcus responded by triumphantly placing his hand atop Theron's. Helghul scowled, looking away, and Theron pulled her hand out from under Marcus's with displeasure. She refused to be a pawn in their rivalry.

"What will the Emissaries do?" another student called out. Yellow Elder felt their doubt and concern and concentrated on projecting comforting energy while responding as specifically as he could.

"The Emissaries will carry forth the sacred knowledge of consciousness as the coming Age becomes dense, and humanity is reborn into darkness. Patience. Soon all of your questions shall be answered. Allow things to flow as they naturally will. That is all," Yellow Elder said. The students were frustrated by the professor's answer.

Yellow Elder exited. He was hesitant to say too much. The students gradually departed, chattering loudly to one another as they made their way to their next lecture or workstation.

As he walked to the White Pyramid, Yellow Elder continued to feel the uncertainty of his students like a thick, humid fog clinging to his every cell. He was heavy with concern about them and their preparedness to become Emissaries.

Have I schooled them as best I could in philosophy, ethics, and higher thinking? Will they be prepared to sacrifice the needs of the individual and the self for the greater good? Will they maintain their connection to one another? All of these questions plagued him, and based on the strong negative energy that had been growing, he knew there wasn't much time.

As Yellow Elder entered the pyramid, all of his senses were inundated. He heard a resounding hum of *"Aum."* He smelled sweet jasmine, and radiant warmth immediately enfolded him like a favorite blanket. He joined the glowing circle that vibrated before him.

The Elders sat, heads bowed, chanting, immersed in meditation. A swirling powerful force circled them, and though they were materially tiny in the vast chamber, they filled the space.

The Elders identified some fear and doubt in the room—a lick of it, a tiny taste, hardly anything compared to the dark fear feeding on itself outside in the private hearts and minds of the Atitalans.

For a moment, darkness erupted, and the inky blackness sent overwhelming doubt and fear through the room into the Emerald Tablet before them, amplifying the negativity. A shadow had entered the pyramid, tipping the balance. The cloaked figure hovered, his shine mingling through the Elders'. Across the compound, Helghul was manifesting darkness, meditating on the fall of Atitala and his rise as Black Elder. Though fear baited them, the Elders continued their meditation and humming.

It was then that the message came clearly to each of the Elders simultaneously: *The Emissaries must depart.*

"We must prepare for the choosing," White Elder said, breaking the circle. Her voice remained calm, though a sense of urgency had gripped them all.

"I pray these Emissaries suffer less than we did," Yellow Elder said.

"Who will accompany the Emissaries?" Orange Elder asked.

"Red and Grey Elder have made the choice to mentor them," White Elder said.

⊱⊰ ⊱⊰ ⊱⊰

Beyond the walls of the White Pyramid, oblivious to the monumental events that were unfolding, Marcus and Theron sat shoulder to shoulder, thigh to thigh, enthralled in conversation on the edge of a turquoise-blue pool. The cenote was a round stone chamber naturally eroded by an underground river, with a number of tunnels branching off into darkness. The fresh water was dazzled by the sunlight springing through the overhead skylight, worn by nature's erosion. Their feet were soothed by the warm, still pool. Roots of living trees hung like chandeliers from the red-soil ceiling, some reaching all the way to the water.

"I love it here," Theron said. "Helghul and I found this place. The first time we came here, we were practicing mind games. One of us used a rock to scrape an image into soil over there, and the other sat here with our feet in the water and tried to guess what it was. I won. He got so mad. He couldn't guess anything I drew." She smiled at the memory.

"How did we misjudge him so completely? We must have ignored the signs," Marcus said, shaking his head and hugging her tightly with one arm.

"He's not so bad, Marcus. He used to be your best friend."

"That was long ago. He was different then," Marcus said, distracted by her thigh pressed firmly against him.

The sun peeking through the open ceiling was splintered by the dangling roots and dappled her in a golden glow. Her nose and her tiny eyes in isolation were nothing special, but somehow, in *her* face, they were perfect. She was reminding Marcus of their many good times with Helghul when he interrupted her.

"The last thing I want to do right now is talk about Helghul," he said, gently placing his hand behind her neck and pulling her in for a deep kiss. She responded willingly, nibbling his bottom lip, and they wrapped their bodies together.

As their passion mounted, she stopped him. She pulled his forehead to meet hers, locking her hands behind his neck, and stayed there with her eyes closed, saying nothing. Marcus felt their connection deeply, and his frustration slipped away. After a moment he stood, without feeling self-conscious, and slipped out of his loose trousers and pulled his tunic over his head, plunging into the welcome cool of the water. As he surfaced, he swam to the edge and searched with his feet for the hollow nook on which to stand.

His caramel skin glistened in the dappled sunlight, and his wavy, soaked hair almost touched his shoulders. Theron stood up and, with one tug, dropped her airy white robe in a heap at her feet. There was only a brief moment before she slipped into the water next to Marcus, but that vision would be forever burned into his memory. It was the single most arousing moment of his life: to see her there, her curves so perfectly long and lean, surrounded by the stunning blue and gold of the cenote. It was almost too much for him.

No amount of cool water could sate him. She came to him, her soft skin pressed against his, her mouth open before their lips met, and their hands explored each other. She felt his hardness against her, and she floated into him. Instantly, she felt the heat between her legs, the longing in her belly. Her second chakra burned while desire shot through her. Marcus's left hand slid tenderly from her hip up to her breast. Her nipple responded to his touch, swelling, and he brought his mouth to it. They held the edge of the pool for support, and her free hand stroked his rippling shoulder. Soon they were kissing again, fevered and wet. Marcus was out of his mind with passion, overwhelmed with his love and longing for her.

"Now," she whispered in his ear, kissing and licking it seductively. Marcus placed his hands on her hips, lifting her as she wrapped her strong limbs around his waist. This was the perfect connection, the ideal moment.

"Stop!" A tortured yell tore through the cave, startling the couple and shattering their blissful state.

The moment gone, they watched in shock as Helghul charged the pool's edge, his eyes wild. "Get away from her!" he ordered. Marcus didn't move, but before he could say anything, Theron shouted at her former friend.

"What are you doing here? Have you lost your mind?" she snapped. Helghul ignored the question and angrily rounded on her.

"You bring *him* to our spot? You spoil our memory with . . . with *him*?" he spat, pacing the edge of the water, glowering at her. His jealousy twisted his thin face, and Theron was stunned by his vehemence.

"You need to leave *now*!" Marcus exclaimed. Theron placed her hand on his shoulder to calm him.

"Helghul, please, just go," Theron said more kindly. Helghul stopped pacing and glared at her, his pale face blotched with rage.

"You are an ugly little nothing! Don't speak to me." Spittle flew as he spoke. He was cut short as Marcus leapt out of the pool, his nakedness forgotten.

Despite Helghul's attempt to back away, Marcus's coiled knuckles crunched against the bone of his cheek. Helghul was thrown back by the blow, his counterpunch lost to the air as he stumbled.

"Stop!" Theron shouted, leaping out of the water. Marcus ignored her as she clutched his bicep, both of them naked and dripping. "Marcus, let go! Let him go!" she shouted. Marcus backed the stumbling adversary to the water's edge and shoved him in.

"What's wrong with you?" Theron said as she began to quickly pull her clothes on.

"You're mad at *me*?" a disbelieving Marcus snapped in response.

"You attacked him, Marcus! You hit him!"

Helghul climbed out of the water, his sopping garments clinging to him. Theron's dress was awkwardly twisted and stuck to her as she instinctively reached out and offered Helghul her hand. As she bent toward him, he did the unthinkable. He backhanded her roughly across the face and sent her reeling on her haunches. Blood flowed from her nose as she skidded across the stone floor, landing with a thump. She was dumbfounded as blood and tears poured down her clinging dress. She had never been hit before. She had never been intentionally injured by *anyone*.

Before Theron could process what had happened, Marcus pounced on Helghul, who was now out of the water. They were wrestling on the ground, and Theron was shouting at them to stop when Helghul unsheathed a knife from the waist of his soaked clothing. He slashed at Marcus, opening a superficial gash in his right forearm. Marcus's eyes bulged at the sight of the weapon. He grappled with Helghul, ultimately sending the blade bouncing off the rock.

"Enough!" A powerful voice boomed through the underground chamber, reverberating off the walls and simultaneously sending a debilitating telepathic screech that cut through their minds painfully. Marcus and Helghul let go of each other, bringing their hands to their ears in useless defense.

Grey Elder stared at the students angrily as they stumbled and pushed away from one another. The young men stood dirty and bleeding, and both avoided the intimidating gaze of the Elder. The older man was tall and extremely thin. He wore his silver hair shaved short, and his dark eyes were stern. His face was red, and his jaw was tightly clenched as he looked at the bloodied, miserable Theron and then back at the young men.

"Grey Elder . . . , " Theron began.

"Say nothing, I have seen enough. I will bring this matter to the Senate," he said. Then, looking at Theron, he added, "Do not let your mother see you thus, Theron. It will distress her unduly."

As Grey Elder looked away, Helghul retrieved his knife and hid it in the folds of his waistband.

Theron marched out of the cavern, regretting that her actions would indirectly reflect on her mother. Marcus bumped against Helghul roughly as he passed to catch up to her. The young men sneered openly at one another, and Grey Elder took Helghul by the arm and steered him away.

"There's no time for your nonsense!" he hissed at the student, and Helghul shook his arm free but stared dejectedly at the ground.

"What made you act that way?" Theron asked, staring at Marcus as they exited the cavern.

"I never felt anger like that before. It completely overtook me."

"Don't you see what's happening? The Golden Age is over. It's more important than ever to resist all negativity. It's only going to get harder!"

Grey Elder was annoyed and deeply troubled. There was so much to do, and the offspring of White Elder only added to his worries. When he arrived back at the White Pyramid, Grey Elder solemnly conveyed the story to the other Elders. White Elder's face clouded with concern, and she asked about Theron.

"What of my daughter? Is she badly injured?" At that moment she was less spiritual leader and more distressed mother.

"She is well, White Elder. She is in her room changing her robes," Grey Elder said.

"This violence on the eve of the choosing . . . what does it mean? Can they be trusted on this odyssey?" Green Elder asked, folding her hands contemplatively.

"Perhaps they are not destined to become Emissaries," Blue Elder said. As the teacher of communications and the dynamics of human behavior and politics, he reminded them how unpredictable people could be.

"We don't know who will be chosen," Red Elder replied.

"We don't have time for this," Grey Elder complained. "The reckoning time has come!"

"Yes, which means valuing our higher self is more important than ever," White Elder reasoned serenely. The Elders joined their hands and bowed their heads, and after a few minutes, they broke apart.

"Be mindful, my friends. The trials will be completed tonight," White Elder said.

As the Elders dispersed, Marcus had taken Theron to her private chamber, and she had quickly bathed and washed the blood away. Her nose had a nasty bruise but was not broken. When she emerged in clean, dry robes, she was aloof and said nothing.

"Something has to be done about Helghul," Marcus said.

"You purposefully harmed another being," she said shortly, fatigue in her voice.

"Me?"

"It's not your fault, it's mine. If we hadn't been there . . ."

"You can't mean that!" Marcus said incredulously. "If Helghul hadn't been sneaking around, none of this would have happened!" He was irritated by her inability to see Helghul realistically.

"You didn't have to attack him. His words didn't hurt me! Be *compassionate*, Marcus! We should both have been more sensitive."

"And the knife, Theron? Is that our fault too?"

"Of course not," she sighed.

Theron had grown used to defending Helghul. Since their experience in Inner Earth, he hadn't been himself, but Theron knew he was misunderstood, and that the boy he used to be must be inside him somewhere. It was more difficult now; he had been so brutal and hateful at the cenote, but she understood that it all came from his own pain. No matter how unintentionally, she and Marcus had hurt him.

Theron turned to leave and, in her haste, did not notice Marcus reaching for her hand.

Chapter 5

The Coupling

Marcus's room was cozy but small, compared to the opulence of Theron's family dwelling, but it was all he required. He tried to clear his thoughts and still his breathing, but images of Theron naked as she had entered the quarry lake, then the cenote, flashed mercilessly through his mind. The tortured young man became aroused beyond comfort at the memory of his love's body standing on the edge of the beautiful water. They had been so close. He was ready. He was so ready he was afraid he would internally combust.

Across the compound at nearly the same time, Helghul had just awakened from a startlingly vivid dream. In it, he had found himself on a precipice in the quarry looking down on Marcus and Theron as they swam. The dream was identical to the events of three moon cycles earlier: every sound, every bird's chirp, down to the rumble of the stones. Helghul witnessed a Nephilim toss a large boulder, inadvertently starting an avalanche.

Helghul once again stood above the desperate, scrambling Marcus, but this time he acted. He did not stay motionless and watch. In his dream, Helghul changed the outcome.

When the rockslide first began, Helghul felt the sensation that he had already been there, that he was in a dream state, and he understood that he could control the flow of the rocks. In his subconscious mind, he had the authority to make the rocks fall or be still. Helghul was intoxicated with his power, and when he saw Marcus and Theron swimming below, he knew exactly what he wanted to do. His conscience beseeched him, but he disregarded the warning.

It's a dream; I cannot be held to account, he reasoned. Helghul released the avalanche and gloried in the destruction. When Marcus clambered onto the rocks, Helghul released a second, more devastating, landslide, crushing his reviled classmate in the rubble below. He stared down at the mayhem that he had unleashed, and he celebrated the supremacy of his will and mind.

Suddenly, he heard a deep male voice say, "Citizen!" and he woke with a jolt.

"Citizen?" he repeated, anxious to learn what the dream meant.

In her chamber, Theron was stretching and contemplating what she would do if Marcus was not chosen. She leaned hard into her slender muscles as they burned and resisted. She remembered the darkness she had seen in Helghul's eyes and the shock she had felt when he had hit her.

Unable to relax, Theron played complex tunes on her harplike instrument, but she plucked the sensitive strings indelicately, and her music was unusually poor, so she laid her instrument aside. The call for the Emissaries coupled with the violence earlier in the cenote turned all thoughts into a brushfire in her head. She meditated, but it was difficult to find serenity. Finally, she retired, exhausted by the day's events.

Theron was not sleeping long before she became aware of her consciousness bursting free of her body. Her shine emerged and separated, and she was indigo-golden light traveling outside of her corpus. Only an ethereal lifeline connected her to her sleeping human form. Like a ribbon, it shimmered and swayed in the starry evening light. Theron stared down at her shell for a moment, awed, as always, to see her body motionless and remarkable as she astral traveled. She willed herself up and out beyond the bounds of the city, and she soared into the night.

Theron heard a familiar voice in her head. It was Marcus. He was speaking to her telepathically. She scanned the star-filled space in excitement; this had never happened before. In the distance she saw his shine, and her heart leapt with joy. Marcus had joined her in astral travel. Their spirits rushed together like solar wind, and they circled one another in greeting and recognition. They were pure energy, and their thoughts flew easily back and forth as the magnificent grid crackled around them, like firing brain synapses.

There were interdimensional beings and other colorful spirits speckling the heavens around them. The feeling of being outside their bodies was thrilling. There was an electric buzzing in their ears, and their physical bodies remained far below them. Theron directed their spirits upward, and together they shed the atmosphere of the Earth, still tethered by glistening, infinite cords to their bodies back home.

Marcus, couple with me now, be my soulmate, for this life and those to come, Theron communicated lovingly. With a thought and an intention, Marcus crossed into Theron and completely immersed his spirit in hers. They did not connect or intertwine; they became one.

Bliss . . . and incredible intensity!

Coupling in the Universal Grid was the ultimate spiritual union, not just the commingling of auras, but the touching and bonding of souls. It was oneness unimaginable in human form— she became him, and he became her. They were fully immersed, unifying energy, and feeling each other absolutely from every perspective. Only material, earthbound creatures had the illusion of separation. Language was inadequate to explain the ecstasy and beauty of their union.

A loud, distinct clash of a gong reverberated through their bound spirits, interrupting them. It was a call to gather, and Theron retreated, causing Marcus's soul to cry out in protest. There was a bright flash, and Marcus's energy flickered but reappeared.

Don't go, he begged.

We need to return, Marcus. The choosing of the Emissaries is near, she said, looking toward home.

Stay with me. This is where we belong. Here, together. We have no reason to ever go back, Marcus insisted.

How will we ever lead others to this place if we keep it for ourselves? Theron answered, and she swiftly made her way to Earth and to her chamber, knowing that Marcus would certainly do the same.

"Marcus, Citizen! Theron, Emissary!" a loud male voice boomed, and Theron woke in her bed with a start.

Had it been a dream? Had they astral-traveled? She could still feel the intense energy of coupling and becoming soulmates with Marcus. She knew it to be true.

Citizen . . . Emissary—she had heard the verdict clearly. Theron trembled at the outcome. She had to talk to Marcus immediately. He could confirm if they had connected or if it had all been a dream, but then she wondered if it mattered. Marcus, Citizen. Theron, Emissary. It could only mean one thing.

Theron jumped up to dress, and rushed out into the glimmering pink sunrise. Marcus was not far away. She had to knock twice before he opened the door, disheveled and bleary-eyed from a night of little sleep.

"Did you astral-travel last night?" Theron blurted out as Marcus led her inside.

"What? No, I don't think so," Marcus said, reaching to push her tangled hair from her face.

"Marcus, either you did or you didn't. You would know!" she snapped impatiently.

"Whoa, what is this? What happened?"

"I had a dream. I think it was a test. It was pass–fail. In the end, you were labeled Citizen, but I was labeled Emissary," Theron said desperately. Marcus looked stricken as he stared at her.

"I failed? Citizen? Why?" he asked.

"You begged me to stay . . . to stay in the grid, and I said no," she said, crying as Marcus put his arms around her and led her to sit on his narrow bed.

"It was a dream, Theron. I wasn't there. I couldn't have failed if I wasn't there," Marcus reasoned.

"Did you . . . have a dream?" Theron asked hopefully. Her green eyes glowed with tears.

"No, I didn't," he said. Theron rested her head on him, unsure what to think. Surely Marcus would not be judged for her dream . . . or would he? What did it mean?

A piercing whistle suddenly pealed through the air, startling the distraught pair and preventing them from ruminating further over her dream. It was time. Theron ran to the door and threw it open. Things had begun to go horribly wrong. She shouted at Marcus to follow her.

Outside, the sky that had been calm and pink minutes earlier had grown dark and sinister while sheets of rain battered the city. Buildings had begun to crumble and fall, and Theron knew that they must get to the wharf as soon as possible. Through the deafening wind and noise, she shouted to him. The couple ran to the port, circling on the curved roads and passing over the canal bridge as it disintegrated behind them and fell into the now-surging channel below. All around them, people were running and yelling, and Theron felt their fear but was unable to help.

When they arrived at the wharf, White Elder was there, ordering students in different directions—some onto the waiting boats and others back toward the Grand Hall. A fork of lightning shattered the ominous sky, and the queue of students trembled as the thunder shook the Earth. The students were soaked through to the skin and shivered as they huddled in the bitter wind, waiting to be sorted.

"Theron, at last. Get on the boat, daughter. Hurry!" White Elder directed.

"Marcus, go back to the hall. I will return there shortly."

"No!" Theron screamed, her eyes wide and disbelieving. "No!"

"He has not been chosen, Theron," White Elder shouted over the din. The winds were increasing, and she crouched slightly to steady herself.

"Stay with me, Theron!" Marcus shouted.

Summoned by a nod from White Elder, four atlantium-powered restraints soared through the air and clamped both his ankles and wrists, disabling him. With a wave of her hand, the atlantium cuffs lifted Marcus and began transporting him back toward the Great Hall. He struggled, slashing his arms and legs futilely through the air.

"Mother, he's my soulmate. Please!" Theron cried out, nearly hysterical as she watched Marcus being carried away from her. She ran to him and grabbed hold of his leg, while he floated, incapacitated by the cuffs.

"You must choose. Will you become an Emissary? There is not much time!" White Elder said as Theron, unable to counter the atlantium that was acting on White Elder's command, stumbled forward, pulled along with Marcus.

"Let go, Theron!" White Elder ordered.

"Don't let go!" Marcus countered.

"Let him join me, please!" Theron beseeched.

"I cannot! He has not been chosen. Will you fulfill your calling to be an Emissary? You must choose!" White Elder commanded as the tempest worsened.

"I have to go!" Theron shouted.

Marcus was stunned, and he looked as though she had punched him. Water ran in thick streams down their faces.

"No! Don't let go!" he cried.

"I must!" she said, her tears hidden by the rain that had soaked them.

Looking into Marcus's heartbroken face, Theron released his leg.

"Emissary!" a deep baritone voice called, and Theron bolted upright in her bed, saved from the torture of her dream. She was soaked from head to toe with sweat, and her tangled hair clung in damp clumps to her skin.

A dream within a dream, she marveled, shaking. She had been chosen as an Emissary. She was certain of that. Theron wondered if Marcus had dreamed, or astral-traveled, or anything at all. Was he still safely asleep across the courtyard in his bed? Had the coupling been real?

Theron looked out the window into the calm, starlit night. It was hours until dawn, and Atitala slept peacefully, but she was unwilling to close her eyes and risk more dreams.

When Marcus finally slept, he had a powerfully vivid dream. He was back in the cenote. This time he was alone. The sun gleamed through the earthen ceiling above him, dancing in silver circles on the still, blue water. Marcus was hot, as if he were sitting in front of a roaring fire rather than in a cool underground cave. The water tempted him, but he felt as though he must not go in. Something inside warned him: a voice, an instinct. Marcus suddenly noticed that there was a water jug dripping with condensation across the beckoning pool.

He was dry with thirst and heat, and finally he stripped down, the muscles of his dark body glistening with sweat. Marcus jumped into the water and felt relief and coolness. As he reached for the jug and brought it to his parched lips, he felt the touch of a gentle hand on his shoulder. In his dream state, he did not need to turn—he knew it was Theron; it was the beautiful girl he loved.

Marcus continued to drink, unquenchable, the jug ever full. Then he felt a hand on his other shoulder that did not quite make sense. He became confused, as one can only be in a dream, and his subconscious struggled to sort it out, but he could not stop drinking the water to look. Finally, he turned, and there were three of them: three beautiful women, each one more beautiful than the next. They were naked and amused, and there was not a large nose or a crooked smile among them.

Their breasts moved seductively as they surrounded him— laughing and smiling—and Marcus could hear music in the distance, his favorite song, and the heat and the thirst that had plagued him was all focused and centered now in his first and second chakras, and his groin felt as though it was on fire. The women were caressing him and kissing him. Marcus ached with desire.

"No," he tried to say, but the words failed to come. He felt the softness of the tiny feminine hands on his body, and they teased him, touching his thighs, his buttocks, and his navel. Coming so close to his tortured organ but never taking hold.

"Do you want us?" one of the women whispered sweetly as she kissed his neck and rubbed her breasts against his arm. He felt them on all sides of him, and he felt their skin, their erect nipples, their bodies so soft and willing. He thought of Theron, and his unconscious mind urged him on: *It's just a dream; she'll never know,* it said.

Marcus battled with himself and knew that he could have them—all of them—if he just stopped resisting, if he just reached out and stroked the soft, warm places between their legs, the beautiful, naked girls in the cenote would be his.

Marcus remembered astral-traveling with Theron and the soul connection he had experienced.

"I have chosen Theron," he said, but the women still clung to him.

"She'll never know," they purred.

"*I'll* know."

The scene changed, suddenly and without reason. Marcus found himself once again walking into the cenote, but this time Theron stood in the distance, removing her filmy robe, her naked body resplendent in the glowing light as she lowered herself into the water. It was just as she had been only hours before, and Marcus was anxious to join her.

Wait! Something is wrong. There was a husky laugh. She was in the arms of a man. A jealous rage welled up in him. Marcus saw Theron lifted up in the water, her legs and arms wrapped lovingly around . . . *him*? He saw himself holding her, his dark head shifting to the side as the couple kissed passionately. It didn't make sense; his emotions surged and burned within him uncontrollably. The dreamer was stunned, his mind scrambling to understand what he was seeing as he inched toward the water's edge. His stomach churned as fury swelled within him.

In the water he saw himself, but no longer himself. He saw the pale face of Helghul looking back at him from his reflection. Confusion. He heard Theron's voice, a faint whisper. "Now," she said, and Marcus's mind exploded in outrage.

"*Stop!*" he shouted. Pain, piercing betrayal, and heartbreak was all he felt. There was no logic, no recollection or understanding that this world was a dream. Marcus was fully engulfed, choking on the bitter scene.

"What are you doing here? Have you lost your mind?" Theron asked.

"You need to leave *now!*" the imitation Marcus shouted.

The dreamer's fury doubled as the imposter jumped out of the water and charged toward him. He felt the cold, hard knuckles against his cheek and was sent reeling backward, his attempt to retaliate lost to the air.

Marcus felt the knife sheathed at his waist, and before his adversary reached him, he pulled it out. Every vessel in his body prepared for battle, and his muscles surged with adrenaline as he stared at the blade in his hand, its handle adorned with ten beastly heads. In his dream's mind, he had changed places with Helghul. He felt the sting of Theron's disregard. He felt the jealousy of her love for the imitation Marcus. The torment of her betrayal was fresh and devastating, fueling the dark passion that had always been latent within him but that had now grown and was eclipsing him.

In that moment of dark anger, Marcus contemplated his predicament. Had Helghul truly felt how he was feeling? Had he been so injured by seeing Theron in Marcus's arms? Marcus was filled with compassion, and he moved through the unconscious rage of his emotion and made a conscious decision. He threw the knife aside and instead prepared only to defend himself. Even in his darkest pain he would not take the life of another.

"Emissary!" a voice boomed.

Marcus jerked awake as if he had dreamed of falling. He lay panting, unable to quiet his racing heart for some time. It had been so vivid, so terribly real. *Emissary,* he thought, understanding that the trial was complete.

Marcus suddenly understood Helghul more fully, having perceived the same situation from his perspective. He pitied his former friend, and though his anger at Helghul for striking Theron remained, it had weakened considerably due to his empathy. Marcus shifted his thinking to the tasks that lay ahead and wondered what they might entail.

Throughout the city, potential Emissaries had meditated and then dreamed realistic and disturbing scenarios that challenged their greatest fears, alliances, and weaknesses. Some were designated Citizen and others Emissary, but each had heard the deep judging tone.

>⊷< >⊷< >⊷<

The sunrise was crisp and fresh, and Theron was knocking on Marcus's door. He opened on the second knock, squinting and bleary-eyed in the bright sun. Theron had the sick feeling of déjà vu as he pulled her inside.

"Did you dream?" she asked anxiously, her eyebrows scrunched with concern.

"I did. Obviously you did too," he said, trying to kiss her as she darted away impatiently.

"Well, what was it?" she asked, barely able to stand the suspense.

"Emissary. Why? What's wrong?" he asked, noticing her crumpled forehead.

"My dream . . . it said you failed . . . I . . . didn't doubt you . . . it was so real, that's all," she stammered.

"I passed," he said, throwing himself down on his bed and making room for her to lie beside him.

"I am so happy we'll do this together," she said, a distracted smile relieving the stress on her face as she sat on the edge of his bed. "I dreamed we coupled in the grid," she added shyly, taking his hand between both of hers.

"It was no dream. It was incredible," he assured her.

"It was real, then? We have become soulmates," she said, delighted that he had experienced it also. It had all been so real . . . but had become so unreal. It was all so confusing.

"I can still feel you."

"Me too," she breathed in relief, lying down next to him and resting silently, forehead to forehead.

After a few minutes, Theron stirred. "I'm going to talk to Mother and see what I can learn. We are to gather in the Senate chamber shortly," she said, kissing Marcus lovingly as she got up.

"Don't go," Marcus said. Theron turned back with a twinkle in her eye and flashed him a smile, but then she slipped out the door and was gone.

Marcus did not rush to dress; instead, he lay in his bed for a long time. He knew he should be thinking about the end of the Age and becoming an Emissary, but all he could think about was the connection with Theron and the energy that had left him vibrating.

Marcus entered the Senate chamber, where Theron was hovering at her mother's elbow. Helghul and his group of cronies were nearby, and Marcus noticed that he avoided looking in the direction of Theron and White Elder. Helghul's eye was purple and black where he had been punched, and Marcus felt shame for his part in it.

"What did you find out?" Marcus whispered conspiratorially, pulling Theron aside.

"Nothing. She completely blocked me. I expected she would."

Helghul glared openly, but Marcus no longer shared his animosity. His experience in the grid with Theron and his cenote experience from Helghul's perspective had changed his smug condescension to empathy. Something must have happened to Helghul in Inner Earth to have changed him so profoundly, and though Marcus wished his friend had confided in him, he also knew that the changes in Helghul, for whatever reason, made friendship impossible.

Directly in front of the spectators was the white marble throne of White Elder. It was massive, and she was dwarfed by it. To the right and left of White Elder were five smaller and less ornate seats.

The hour had arrived, and all of the potential students had been gathered. The Elders—Red, Grey, Yellow, Orange, Blue, and Green—took their seats. White Elder addressed them effectively, with only the amplification of the well-designed room to help.

"Welcome. You are a worthy, courageous group, and any one of you would make an honorable Emissary. What you must remember is that for each of you there is a plan. If it is not your path to become an Emissary, it is not a shame upon you or a fault. It is simply not your calling. Last night in your dreams, the trials were completed; and you faced your fears, your weaknesses, and your desires. There are those of you who are destined to become Emissaries . . . and those who are not. If you have been chosen, you clearly heard the decree of 'Emissary.' If you heard the verdict 'Citizen,' there is no dishonor. Many good people will stay here in Atitala."

Marcus and Theron began whispering as students all around them reacted in a noisy assortment of emotions.

"Citizens, please return to your homes and families now, and pray for your compatriots as they journey forth," White Elder instructed. Scores of people embraced, cried, and offered encouragement, while many others skulked from the room, downcast and disappointed despite White Elder's assurances.

The crowd thinned less than Marcus had first anticipated; Bapoo and Yashoda were among the thousands remaining in the rows. Marcus was astonished to see that Helghul was still there. White Elder spoke again as the last of the eliminated students exited.

"It is time for all of you to understand the role of the Emissaries, and the difficulty and sacrifice that this choice will bring. Divisiveness, doubt, and fear will cause chaos and seek to consume each spirit in the primitive world that will eventually emerge. We must bring balance. We must ensure that the Emerald Tablet's message, which was passed on to us from our ancestors, is not forgotten.

"Take the knowledge you have been given and weave it through the fabric of the new world—in its art, music, architecture, and mathematics. Let those who would ask, find the clues and the way back to Oneness. It is your destiny as the chosen ones to keep hope, truth, and virtue alive in the world. We are all one consciousness. Without goodness there is only darkness. Without the darkness one cannot choose the light."

The audience stirred, and Marcus looked at Helghul, who sat with his arms crossed. He did not understand how Helghul could be a chosen one, but as the question occurred to him, Marcus's inner voice reminded him that he, too, was flawed.

White Elder took her seat as Green Elder stood. The stocky woman walked to the forefront, not much taller standing than when sitting. Her thick head sat directly on her shoulders with no sense of a neck at all, but her broad, flat face was warm and loving.

"As you go forward, you will live among the people as equals. You will die and be reborn. Though it will not be easy, you will always embody your true nature, and your intuition and third eye will remain conscious and perceptive. You have each been carefully chosen as Emissaries; it is your destiny, if you choose it."

"What will happen to Atitala and her people in this time of chaos?" Solenna asked from beside Helghul.

"The citizens of Atitala will follow their own path," White Elder replied.

"If we go, can we return? Will we see our families again?" Yashoda asked.

"You will commit to the entire cycle of the Great Year. You will not return to Atitala, though your soul groups will support you," Green Elder said simply, referring to the way souls clustered with one another as they incarnated, helping one another to evolve.

"When do we depart?"

"You will depart when the sun reaches its zenith at midday tomorrow. The vessels are prepared at the wharf. Red and Grey

Elder will accompany you to guide and mentor you over the Ages," White Elder said.

The room erupted with conversation. Boats? So soon? And never to return! How could they decide something so serious so quickly?

Tomorrow! Marcus telegraphed to Theron. Her eyebrows were creased together. Her mind was occupied with the sadness of leaving her mother the very next day. Theron could not imagine being without her as a spiritual compass to guide her.

"Why boats?" a student asked.

"Simplicity is best when future resources and technology are uncertain. A boat's form lends itself easily to function and understanding in primitive times," Yellow Elder explained.

"Will we know each other?" Marcus asked, cutting through the din. White Elder found his face in the crowd and searched his eyes knowingly.

"No. In each incarnation, you will be born without memory. Your choices will create your future experiences," White Elder said. The room was no longer silent as the potential Emissaries whispered and mumbled to one another.

Marcus. We're soulmates. We will find one another, Theron projected, understanding his concern.

"Those of you who choose to fulfill this destiny and to function as keepers of the knowledge shall not remember your ties to Atitala. At each birth you will be free of past memory, free of memories that would cause feelings of loss, despair, and longing. You will be reincarnated to share your inner light and virtue with the world. Let this be clear to you all—once you die and are reborn in the world of humankind, your only memory will be of your purpose, your sense of duty . . . and you will carry that with you always," Yellow Elder said.

The room again erupted in conversation. White Elder's voice called for silence, and the fervor quieted.

"Now, understanding the undertaking, those who will choose to be Emissaries should stay. If you choose to stay in Atitala, you may leave," she said.

All around Marcus and Theron, their classmates were in varied states of emotional uproar. Theron saw Helghul at the edge of the room and tried to catch his eye. She wanted to make peace. She wanted him to know that she was glad that he had passed the trials and been called to be an Emissary. It confirmed for her that the goodness she had known was within him. Helghul purposefully avoided Theron's gaze, and once more his resentment saddened her.

Not everyone who was declared an Emissary was prepared to sacrifice and leave the next day forever. Students began filing out of the hall. Some walked proudly, while others slipped from the room.

"What if we stay here?" Marcus asked.

"Marcus!"

"I don't want to forget you."

"We're soulmates; we can never be truly separated. We have to go, Marcus . . . we're meant to go," she replied. Marcus knew she was right.

Marcus saw Helghul loitering at the edge of the crowd, surrounded by a small group.

"I can't believe he's an Emissary," Marcus said, changing the subject and nodding in Helghul's direction.

"He's as much a part of the unity as we are," Theron replied.

"It is time to choose. Emissaries, please join us at the front of the hall for the commitment oath," Orange Elder announced.

The Elders stood spaced equally apart, and the students assembled in orderly lines in front of them. One by one, the students took their places in front of the leaders. Placing their right hands to their hearts while their left hands were embraced by the Elder in front of them at their wrists, they repeated the vows given to them:

"I choose to become an Emissary. I promise to share the truth of oneness and to ease the suffering throughout the trials of the Great Year. I will keep alive the knowledge that illuminates the pathway to enlightenment and consciousness."

The Emissaries were then embraced and blessed and dismissed one by one. The vows were powerful, and many were overcome with emotion, purified by the process.

From his place in line, Marcus searched the chamber for Helghul's flaxen head but could not find him. *Has he already pledged and left?* Marcus wondered curiously, still skeptical that his former friend had been chosen at all. Marcus was scanning the room when Theron nudged him forward to face White Elder.

"Have you made a choice, Marcus?" White Elder asked, studying the young man's face carefully.

"I choose to accept my role as Emissary."

White Elder took hold of Marcus's left wrist, reciting the vow. Marcus repeated the words and felt the overwhelming joy of the cleansing, but at the same time he felt a weight—the weight of a task too large for him.

As he waited for Theron to take her vow, Marcus humbly wondered if he was up to the assignment ahead.

"Theron, I am happy for you," White Elder said, kissing her forehead.

"Yes, Mother, but I am heartsick to leave you," she said. White Elder did not reply, but instead, as she had done to the others, she took Theron's left wrist. Theron marveled at the tender touch, her wonderful, gentle hands. She knew them so well.

White Elder looked into her daughter's green eyes as Theron recited her vows in a powerful, clear voice. "I hope that you will join me for a walk . . . alone," White Elder requested. "I will fetch you from your chamber in two hours."

"Of course." Theron smiled. She was thrilled to be set apart and craved her mother's undivided attention.

"Let's go," Theron said, taking Marcus's hand. He joined step with her, grateful at the prospect of being alone.

When they arrived at her quarters, a fire had been lit, and a variety of delicious food had been laid out. The couple rested together on a wide settee, with her head on his chest. They alternately kissed, sipped wine, and discussed their future.

"We can still have our life wherever we end up," Marcus said. "We can do everything, just in a new place."

"I hope so." Theron smiled. "I sense that we're going to carry a heavy load."

"I can still feel you. As if you're in my blood, surging through me," he said, as she nestled against his neck.

She looked up into his eyes. "Coupling was more than I imagined. There is so much awareness."

"Now we're connected . . . forever," he said.

"Forever."

Marcus looked down at her. Her eyelids were heavy and full of passion, and he pulled her to him. He kissed her deeply and turned his body to meet hers directly. She felt his excitement, and it increased as she pushed as close to him as she could. They kissed and touched eagerly through their clothing, his hand rubbing and urging her on. She stroked his chest and ran her hand firmly down his body, stopping between his legs and holding him, so excited, so ready.

Theron released him and slowly moved away. She stood up, and he reached out to stop her. She tenderly moved his hands away, crossed her arms in front of her, and took hold of her robe by either hip. She pulled the garment easily over her head, and the action lifted her thick, dark hair and sent it cascading down her naked shoulders.

She smiled down at him, the firelight licking her freckled skin, just as he desired to do. He feverishly reached out to touch her. He sat on the edge of the settee now, his hands on her hips. She stood in front of him, and he pressed his lips to the flat, soft skin of her belly. He moved down, kissing, licking, and pleasing her. She made small sounds, her breath quickening, her hands stroking his hair and shoulders.

Their energy was undeniable and eternally connected. They shifted to her bed, kissing lovingly and holding each other tightly so that their skin touched in every way possible. They moaned in pleasure as he entered her for the first time.

They found themselves exactly in the moment, not worried about the past or future. She opened her eyes and—*whoosh!*—there was a tug right at the core of her. He felt it too, and their spirits and energies mingled and twisted, remembering each other. He wanted to stay there forever, to make it last forever.

"I love you," he said.

"I love you," she answered. They knew that they had always known each other. She wrapped herself around him and sent her soul deliberately, deeply, into him. She felt his colors reaching back to her, sending her everything. They stayed close, touching long after the climax had come and gone. She took his hand and brought his inner wrist to her lips.

"This kiss holds all my love for you, my dreams for us." She rested her petal-soft lips gently against him, and he cradled her closely with his other arm. The lovers lay together, their bodies entwined—feet, arms, legs. So grateful to have their skin touching.

Theron soon fell asleep, her soft breath against his neck. He lay still, not wanting to wake her, and watched the firelight dance across her angular face. A light knock at the door interrupted his reverie, and Theron stirred groggily and then jumped to attention.

"Oh, Marcus! You let me sleep!" she scolded in a whisper, as she grabbed her discarded robe and pulled it over her head. "Marcus, she'll see you!"

"She knows we're together, Theron," Marcus whispered, pulling on his pants. White Elder knocked at the chamber door more insistently, and a disheveled Theron slipped out, apologizing to White Elder, who looked through the crack and saw Marcus half-dressed.

With the mother and dutiful daughter gone, Marcus dressed and walked to the courtyard surrounding the Grand Hall. He saw some of the other Emissaries, and they were vibrating with excitement. His apprehension continued to mount, and he saw the heavy burden they carried, even if they did not.

As Marcus walked, he saw Helghul and noticed that he was heading in the direction opposite of his own home.

What's he up to now, always slinking about? Marcus wondered. Spontaneously, his intuition tingling and having no other interest to occupy him, he decided to follow.

Marcus was cautious, remembering the episode with the knife, and not certain how unpredictable Helghul might be. More than once, Marcus was almost noticed: first, walking across the central canal bridge when there was little to camouflage him; and then again while running behind his classmate through the jungle. Marcus was careful to avoid detection as he followed Helghul out of the city and ultimately to the caves beyond the quarry.

Marcus deduced that Helghul was returning to the tunnels. Was he hoping to somehow access the fire lines and escape to Inner Earth? The young man's body pulsated with curiosity and adrenaline as he passed the location where Theron had almost drowned. He was certain that Helghul was hiding something.

Chapter 6

The Exodus; Conjuring Darkness

Marcus had to move quickly to keep Helghul in sight as his rival navigated expertly through the labyrinth of tunnels and caves in the mountainside. They had passed the glowing cenote as they delved deeper into the Earth. Innumerable colonies of bats slept, squeaked, and flew through the caverns. Marcus flinched as a silky wing brushed his cheek.

The smell of bat feces was overwhelming, and Marcus covered his mouth and nose in disgust. He tried to keep his steps as soundless as possible and was aware of the movement and life skittering around him in the darkness. Helghul's light source disappeared ahead many times, and Marcus had almost become lost in the overwhelming obscurity more than once. He listened for Helghul's footfalls and cursed his own unpreparedness.

As they wound deeper into the rocky maze, Marcus grew concerned. He had never explored this far. What if he got lost? What if Helghul had seen him and was leading him into a trap? How would he find his way out? Who knew what danger might lie ahead or what creature he could encounter? He was rushing to keep pace and held his arm bent over his head at eye level to warn of rock outcroppings since the light was almost always only a flicker turning through the low, narrow passageway in the distance. He was almost bent in half and wondered if he should turn back from this reckless pursuit.

The tunnel narrowed further, and Marcus hurried as Helghul disappeared through a ridiculously small opening approximately two yards up the wall. Marcus pressed his body against the stone and found foot- and handholds. He then boosted himself up and cautiously emerged through the opening, which was only just large enough to allow his broad shoulders entry.

Marcus pulled himself up and was standing on a steep precipice. Below him was an open, circular pit that likely had an entrance from the other side of the mountain. It had obviously once been excavated. Firelight, cast by five large torches evenly spaced around the circumference, danced in the shadows of the hollowed cavern.

Marcus heard the murmur of voices, and as his eyes traveled down the cave walls, he was stunned to see the unusual and substantial congregation gathered below. Beneath each of the torches stood an enormous Nephilim looking menacing in extravagant leather armor braided with silver and gold.

There were hundreds of people, including Helghul, and Marcus recognized most of them. He saw Solenna, one of the girls who had helped them distract the Nephilim. She did not appear to be afraid of the giant standing behind her now. He wondered which of them had been chosen as Emissaries, if any, and what business they could possibly have in this pit.

Helghul obviously had a position of importance among the group. As he passed, each individual bowed or nodded to him in respect. On his order, the group began to chant, focusing on the chromatic notes. The inharmonious chant grated on Marcus, and he rolled his head on his neck to shake out the tension that had gathered in his body. He gritted his teeth as the dark intonation continued and grew louder. He had never heard anything like the hum that vibrated through him, the air, and the Earth, reaching the darkness just below.

Marcus's instincts were that he should flee, but his curiosity would not permit it. He was determined to see what Helghul was up to. It was a decision he would eventually regret . . . many times over.

Suddenly, the eavesdropper's attention was drawn by a burst of light to the opening through which he had just come. Marcus shifted as far as he could away from the hole and found a generous outcropping in the dark wall. Silently, he cursed his white pants and tunic, aware that his brown skin would camouflage him much more effectively. He tucked himself out of sight as best he could, his belly flat against the ridge, knowing that it wouldn't hide his brawny frame if anyone shone a light directly at him. He saw a slender hand reach up through the opening, and his heart hammered in his chest as he prepared to fight or run.

The figure passed within two yards of him, and as Marcus had hoped, the individual's attention and light source had been fixed on the spectacle and sound below. He was not discovered. Marcus released the air slowly from his lungs as the newcomer joined the others in the hollow.

The new arrival was obviously in charge and wore a heavy, dark cloak. Marcus regretted that he hadn't dared to look as the stranger had passed. He was desperate to know who had convened a group of students in such an unlikely place. The ringleader's voice suddenly boomed through the eerie vibration of voices. It quivered strangely, and Marcus could not place it. The glow of the torches flickered as a hot wind was conjured and twisted up from the center of the circle. Before he had time to think, a ceremony had begun.

"Shadows empower your disciples. Your servants will go forward and be the Adversaries to the Emissaries, shifting the balance in the coming Ages and teaching the lessons that must be learned. The Golden Age has ended. Let the Darkness be reborn," the deep voice roared, as the chanting continued and grew louder.

Was this Black Elder? Had he returned?

Marcus's intuition beseeched him to flee, but he would not. His need to understand could not be overcome by fear or common sense, and he stood mesmerized as a scene of horror and carnage unfolded at lightning speed below him.

"We bring the innocents at this time of decline, this time of change, and we sacrifice them to you freely," the voice continued. The ring of students was circling, swaying, and jerking as if in a trance. The Nephilim, who had thus far stood silently observing beneath the five points of light around the room, disappeared to a corner of the cavern that Marcus could not see. Marcus could vaguely hear the squawk of creatures, perhaps birds, but the dark hymn was so loud that he could not be sure.

The fervor of the chanting group doubled, and their movements became frantic as the Nephilim returned to their posts beneath the torches. Marcus struggled to comprehend the scene. With horror, he realized that each of the giants held a flailing, squirming child. The indifferent Nephilim held the screaming babes like sacks in front of them and roughly passed them to members of the macabre circle.

I have to do something! What is this? Marcus thought in panic. Nothing in his life in Atitala had prepared him for this. In the brief second it took Marcus to compose a single coherent thought, it was too late to intervene, though it would have been useless to try.

Without warning, or further ceremony, the central leader raised his hands into the air and shouted, "Rise now, Darkness. Accept this sacrifice!" The toddlers were mercilessly swung against the cave walls as if they were mats to be beaten clean. Marcus dropped to his knees in shock, and a powerful howl inexorably escaped him and was swallowed easily by the noise below.

Too late, Marcus turned his face away; what he had witnessed could not be unseen. He retched over and over, vomiting in the dirt as he sobbed uncontrollably. The Nephilim had each taken up a wide drum, and they began to beat in rapid pulse, urging the humans on. Marcus rocked back and forth in horror, his eyes clamped tightly closed, unable to stop the retching that wracked his body.

The chanting continued, heightened by the carnage. Marcus dared not look. He did not want to see the gore; he could not fathom the violation of Divine laws, the inhuman sacrifice of the innocent. He felt the evil grow exponentially around him, and he shivered and cried in horror. He wanted to disappear, to be anywhere other than where he was, and the burden of guilt was quick to envelop him. He should have done something! Anything! The innocent blood indelibly stained Marcus's soul. He had witnessed humanity at its darkest.

Again, the master began to speak, and Marcus trembled, immobile and forever changed. He dared to look again just as Helghul moved to the center of the feverish, chanting circle. The student had removed his tunic and stood only in trousers; his lean torso trembled in anticipation, and his pale skin glowed orange in the firelight. The females in the group churned and danced as if entranced; still chanting, they discarded their robes. Their varied shapes and movements, their exposed flesh, fed the perverse energy that was building in the room.

The Nephilim watched eagerly as the leader directed the many women. They placed their hands on Helghul's waiting body. They kissed him and licked him, clutching and rubbing. There was no part of him unmolested, and the sexual energy of the rite raised the fervor of the group.

The cloaked master never joined, but directed the men in the outer circle to fall in upon the women in a base frenzy of sexual chaos: a reward for their allegiance. The Nephilim shouted and cheered in depraved appreciation. The remnants of bloodied white robes and tunics were torn away as the Adversaries' bodies became alive with the burning, compelling power of the lower-chakra impulses; and they violently coupled, sodomized, and fornicated in every combination possible. Their unquenchable sexual desire was the hold over them. Lust was an age-old influence and power that had led many to the darkness with its promise of pleasure. Their further wish for power, notoriety, and material reward had led each of them to the cavern.

The drumming continued, but the chanting had been replaced by guttural grunts and cries and moans and, more ominously, the sound of distant thunder. It was so far from the experience Marcus had shared with Theron only hours earlier. Helghul was at the center of the rite, shaking in twisted orgasm, when the leader shouted above the din.

"It is time for the initiate to become the host. The soul who will be offered to the dark entity stands willingly before us. Power will be yours!" the leader declared, and the group broke their chant and echoed him.

"Power will be ours!" they bellowed, robotically separating from one another and returning to their circle. When the drumming suddenly ended, Marcus could clearly hear the rumble of thunder, and an ominous distant roar.

Get out! Marcus's inner voice shouted in warning. He was overwhelmed by the feeling of impending doom that pressed his already overfilled senses. He was in shock, and there was no power in him to run away.

The leader began to speak in a strange language that Marcus did not recognize. The naked group continued to sway hypnotically as if drugged, as they began once again to chant, sweat soaking their bodies. As he spoke, the cloaked man circled Helghul with the knife brought back from Inner Earth. The younger man stood fearlessly, waiting with his arms outstretched.

Helghul's face was turned boldly skyward, and he looked weirdly euphoric. Dark powers and ambitions not seen for many millennia were being called upon.

The sinister master brought the knife down, resting the glinting blade against the flesh of Helghul's left forearm. Though Marcus's hatred for his adversary burned like never before, he did not wish to see his murder.

The master began to speak:

"Hear me now, Darkness of the night
Chained in the fetters of fire by Light
Reach now forth this sacred land
Misbegotten beast take now this offered hand
See me now, oh wicked eye
Seek this place from whence we die
Offer this, your sacred feast
Rise up now, all-powerful beast!"

On the final syllable, the leader handed Helghul the handle depicting the ten-headed beast. It was the same blade Helghul had used to cut Marcus in the cenote, and the young man now willingly slashed open his own forearm. His blood spurted across the dirt, and a jagged crevice opened up in the ground, expanding deeper and wider where the crimson trail had fallen. There was a deviant howl from the Earth as her solid bedrock was painfully divided by the deliberate actions of the humans. With a loud crack, the rock bed beneath Helghul's feet split open.

Marcus prayed desperately, begging for divine intervention and sending light and positive energy into the cavern below. Marcus's single light was not enough, and the shadows and dark energy continued to spew forth. Repeatedly, the vast chamber filled, and the Darkness moved easily through the walls, released into the world beyond.

Marcus trembled as a terrifying demonic presence emerged from the chasm like cruel afterbirth and filled the chamber. The ten-headed, dragon-like beast flickered, both particles and wave. It was an ominous grey, purple, and blue, like a bruise. The evil presence gnashed its jagged fangs, howling at the mesmerized group as they chanted and reveled in the dark vibration.

"O Brother, how great thy will be, son of man, son of man. Who is there among you who would open the door, this door that accepts the offering at my hand?" The Beast spoke in a cacophony of rumbling tones from every head at once.

Helghul, formerly brave and defiant, inwardly shuddered at the sight of it. It was more horrible than he had imagined, more horrible than his worst nightmare, and his passionate fervor was replaced by cold dread. Denying his fear, he lifted his head proudly, drawing on the envy and admiration of the adoring assembly. He was the chosen one, the Black Elder, and he offered up his bloody arm.

"I do!" he shouted. Ten heads and twenty fiery eyes snapped to look at him at once, and without another word, the wraith entered Helghul like a drug through a syringe. It infiltrated his veins through his bloody, self-inflicted wound, and Helghul screamed in agony as his body was lifted a yard off the ground. He jerked and jolted violently, defying gravity in the center of the circle and hovering over the endless crevice. The torches on all sides of the room grew brighter, highlighting Helghul's contorted face.

As the evil took hold, Helghul did not resist. He was no longer solely in charge of himself. He had combined with the Beast. He was now a human incubator—this act alienated the natural material world.

As the membrane between worlds had been successfully breached, fractures had opened, and the underworld had been freed of its confines. Shadows moved through the cavern—not cast by fire or form but with their own will and way. They were less powerful dark entities, newly released with the Beast, and they flew among the people below, mingling with them.

As the Ages descended, separation and self-interest would reign. The physical world would be misunderstood as humankind grew more self-important, forgetting its equanimity and connection to everything else.

The new Helghul growled in twisted ecstasy. The transfer was complete. Helghul stood on his feet, a welcoming host to the darkness, with the ten-headed beast concealed within. The King of the Adversaries had been ordained as Black Elder.

The cloaked leader signaled an end to the chanting. "We have succeeded. Through Helghul, we have opened the gate to the Darkness; the cycle has shifted. Our strength will soar as the Ages decline. The Emissaries must not succeed in bringing enlightenment to this new world. You, among others, will be the instruments of discord. Consciousness will become a myth, a lie, blasphemy to speak of. As the Ages darken, people will forget. Adversaries, depart! Spread fear, isolation, and doubt; and by all means, control the weak. Keep their frequencies low and feeble."

The speaker was interrupted by the groan of shifting Earth.

"There is no time left. You must all get to the wharf! There is no time to lose!" Awakened from a deep hypnotic state, the students jerked upright, scrambling to dress.

"We have not been chosen as Emissaries. How will we board the boats?" one of the Adversaries called out.

"The passage of the Adversaries is assured. The universal balance guarantees it. Like the Emissaries, you have chosen your path."

The Adversaries departed for the wharf. They were not the possessed, mechanistic assembly from moments before. They showed no remorse or shock, but rushed purposefully toward the waiting boats. The Nephilim were dismissed and filed out of the cave, their lust for violence fulfilled.

"Take the east exit. Everyone hurry to the boats!"

Marcus heard the urgings of the dark leader, and knew that he, too, must hurry and get to Theron. The Emissaries must depart now, not tomorrow, as they had been told, but it was too dangerous for him to move. Helghul was now alone with the grand master, and Marcus tried to see who was hidden beneath the dark cloak, but his hood remained in place.

"Helghul, you have done well. You will go on to live many lives of great consequence."

"I feel even greater power within me—it's intoxicating—but strangely, I still feel myself," Helghul answered.

"You are yourself, but more. You are intertwined with a powerful ally, and your purpose is deeply embedded. Though your
avatar will be born and die, your spirit is united with the power,
and it will remain attached to you in every incarnation. Remember, though you may feel it, you are not invincible. Do not waste
your lifetimes; think strategically. Before you go . . . I have an
elixir that will grant you past-life memory. The potion will assure
that when you reincarnate, one lifetime to another, you will have
memory—an advantage the Emissaries will not have."

"Why would you not give it to all of us?" Helghul asked. Marcus had just been wondering the same thing and cringed, thinking that he had shared a thought with the monster.

"Because it gives one too much power. Power must be carefully
protected . . . if it is shared, it ceases to exist."

"But why, then, did White Elder not give it to her Emissaries
to empower them?"

"Because of her weakness and compassion—memory is a cruel
burden she would not impart. She believes each lifetime must be
a journey to enlightenment as intended, even for the chosen ones
. . . even in the darkest times."

Marcus was enraged that Helghul would have the advantage
of memory, and the Emissaries would not. He thought, *If there is a
memory elixir, we should all have it. The Emissaries could do far more
good, couldn't they? It would allow Theron and me to remember each
other.* He knew he had to talk to White Elder and convince her.

The cloaked man handed a small bottle to Helghul, who duti-
fully drank it and then tossed the container to the ground. Then,
the two men quickly moved out of Marcus's sight. They had taken
another exit. Marcus waited, nauseated and distraught from everything he had witnessed. He was desperate to get to Theron and to
inform White Elder of what he had seen and seek the memory
potion, but he feared that time was running out.

Once he was sure that the two men were gone, Marcus moved.
Three of the five torches below were still burning, and though
Marcus still trembled, loathing the idea of descending into the
grotesque chamber below, he knew that he needed light to get out

of the cavern. He stealthily descended the stone steps and jumped the crevice with a shudder, remembering the darkness he had seen and felt pouring from it. He approached the stained wall, intentionally averting his eyes. He knew he would be unable to function if he looked down or thought or remembered, so he pushed the reality of the carnage he had witnessed from his mind and focused on speed and survival.

Marcus had to jump to dislodge a torch—it dropped on his third attempt, landing with a thud as he leapt sideways so he wouldn't get burned. He bent to retrieve the light and saw a silver flask discarded on the floor: the memory elixir. He retrieved the bottle and saw that it was not empty. There was a trace still in the bottom, perhaps enough for one.

Stop! his mind warned. All around him, the ground shook, and he covered his head as dust and rubble fell from the ceiling. *Time, time!* There was no time. He knew he had to choose.

This elixir is a gift, he told himself. *This must be why I am here. I can't forget what Helghul has become. I can't forget* her, he thought as he put the vial to his lips and drained it. Marcus had chosen to become an Emissary with Theron, but now he had chosen to do this on his own terms.

The potion tasted of eucalyptus and mint and something bitter that he couldn't place. Marcus stared at his hands, expecting them to change visibly before his eyes. The potion bound itself to every molecule of his DNA, stripping the insulation and respite his spirit might have known and replacing it with the burden of knowledge. Like Helghul, Marcus had chosen a path of full memory, and he would struggle many lifetimes with the consequences of that choice.

Again, the ground rumbled and quaked, and fire joined the fury. From the deep regions of Inner Earth, boiling lava bubbled up, overflowing the crevice that had been broken open by the Beast. Hissing sparks shot into the air, and Marcus tossed the bottle and got out of the cavern as quickly as possible. When he finally emerged from the deep recesses of the mountain, nauseated and terrified, the weather had deteriorated. The sky was dark and foreboding. Stinging rain punished his exposed skin, and the wind howled as trees crashed down around him.

Marcus ran in desperation toward Theron's home. Theron opened the door expectantly at his first frantic knock.

"Did you hear the call?" she asked nervously. She quickly picked up her heavy cloak and pulled it over her head.

"What? No. Theron, we have to find your mother!" Marcus exclaimed, barely able to keep from breaking down at the sight of her; his senses had been pushed too far. Marcus dripped puddles all over her floor, but neither of them noticed. He couldn't bear to tell her what he had witnessed. He didn't want to burden her, and he didn't want to break down. He knew he had to inform White Elder.

"We need to go to the boats right away! My mother will find us!" she said. Theron was across the room, putting on her sandals. "Come on!" she urged impatiently, and Marcus had no will but to follow. The tempest howled outside, loud and ominous.

"We have to find White Elder!" Marcus insisted as they ran. She looked at him, bewildered.

"Do you think this is easy for me . . . leaving her?" she asked. "We have no more time!" She reached back to him. He took her hand, and they ran together. Strange winds whistled through the building, and when they opened the outer doors, Theron was shocked. A gale howled, rocking the vast island with its fury. Hard pellets of hail and rain pitched against them. The pair raised their arms to shield their faces. Marcus knew why darkness had come so quickly.

"Hurry!" Marcus urged, desperate to get himself and Theron safely on a boat. All around them, the noise was deafening. Trees were whipped like blades of grass, and they heard the loud crack and snap of breaking wood. Things were getting worse.

Marcus and Theron were soaked to the skin now. As they neared the wharf, Marcus wondered if the boats could survive the anger and chop of the surf that was pounding them. He wondered how they could possibly get away safely. Marcus saw a steady stream of people braving the stormy darkness. All around him drenched, determined Emissaries were making their individual treks to the boats.

Ahead, he could see Green Elder and Red Elder frantically loading the boats, and he wondered where the other Elders were at that critical moment. Marcus was determined to tell White Elder what he had witnessed in the cavern before he embarked. Hunched against the towering tidal spray and burning wind, the horde of students cowered as a blinding flash tore open the angry sky and a lightning strike met the Earth with a violent blow. The Earth cracked, lava and fire erupted, separating the city and buildings from the beach and wharf. The ground began to shake, first gently like a mother soothing her child, but quickly becoming a violent, rocking force.

A deafening thunderclap rolled, and calm rapidly became chaos as the citizens of Atitala panicked. A wall of fire rose, shielding the fleeing Emissaries from the frightened throng of Atitalans surging to join them at the water's edge.

"Remember, you are eternal," a familiar female voice rang out. "This is a time of transition and transcendence. We are One," she continued, somehow audible above the violent wind and thunder. Marcus searched the landscape to find the source of the ministry, and there, on the wrong side of the wall of fire, he saw White Elder.

The good leader was calling the faithful people of Atitala to her, soothing them. Marcus knew that he would never have a chance to inform White Elder of what he had witnessed. The Earth's floor shifted and moaned as if alive.

White Elder stood calmly, hands and face lifted to the pouring sky, surrounded by organized circles of men, women, and children linking arms or hands and chanting a steady beat and hum in the glowing light of the massive fire. Most of the people of Atitala were merging, facing the trial with faith and acceptance as they had been taught, but not all of the Atitalans chose to join with the others; some embraced fear.

The departing Emissaries watched in horror as some of their fellow citizens ran desperately into the vicious fire, trying to escape and reach the boats, but instead, unable to make it through, they burned, screamed, and died a horrible death. The Emissaries were helpless and distraught but continued purposefully to board the waiting vessels.

Marcus and Theron were getting close to the wharf when another voice cut through the roaring night.

"Help me!" it called. "Someone, please help me!" Marcus heard the shouting. He and Theron were only a hundred yards from one of the launch points. Most of the massive reed boats had already departed. The ground continued to bend and shift; wind and rain beat down on the Emissaries.

"Help me, please!" the voice called out again. Marcus looked back just as Grey Elder, limping, broke through the tall grass, his face contorted with pain. There were only moments left; he had to decide. Theron drove forward through the storm, and it was certain that she would meet their destination. They were only ten yards from the gangplank.

"Please, Marcus, help me!" Grey Elder called, limping faster toward the wharf. They were nearly there, and Marcus made up his mind. He let go of Theron's hand.

"I'll be right back—go on!" he shouted. She understood and lowered her head against the weather. He turned and sprinted back the hundred yards across the shaking ground to help the older man. He wrapped his arm under Grey Elder's own, and they turned back toward the boats.

Beaten by the rain, wind, and spray, Theron turned just in time to see them lift the gangplank, struggling in the brutal conditions to pull it in.

"No!" she shouted, running to stop them. "You have to wait—he's coming!" Her voice was lost in the storm, and the reed boat was already pulling away. Theron heard a voice, a powerful reminder within her that told her to remember her purpose, but her connection to Marcus was too overpowering, and she was determined to stay with him. They would catch another boat. She sprinted to jump the three-foot gap over the water back to the wharf. She knew there was another boat; she and Marcus would take the last one together. Just as she leapt, a strong arm swung out to stop her and grabbed her in midair. She was held from behind by the waist while she struggled.

"Let me go! I have to go back!" she shouted, but the grip was relentless, and the gap between the wharf and the boat grew—five, twenty, a hundred yards—and a wave lifted and carried them beyond chance.

Marcus watched from the shore, running and fully carrying Grey Elder. The boat had pulled away, and he had seen his Theron running to come back to him. He had watched as she collapsed, the boat too far to reach. Helghul held her snugly, not loosening his grip as she fell helplessly to her knees. From behind her, he smiled triumphantly as Marcus charged the dock, releasing Grey Elder. Helghul watched his rival, who stood on the shore shouting, flailing, arms outstretched uselessly reaching to sea. Marcus's pain and anger were lost in the night.

Marcus watched as Theron's ship was tossed and carried farther away. He howled in anguish, and his heart exploded to pieces in his chest.

"I am so sorry, my son," Grey Elder offered. Marcus couldn't hear him, couldn't see, and couldn't fathom anything but his blinding pain.

"She's gone! I've lost her," he said, unable to stem the tide of his grief.

"This is the last boat, Marcus; you can find Theron when we reach our destination. We have to get on the boat, Marcus! If she is on a ship, you can find her when we land! Marcus, this is your only hope!" he bellowed.

Marcus carried the Elder down the wharf to the last remaining boat. Struggling to balance as he traversed the quaking ground, they finally made it. They were the last to board, and the gangplank snapped and was swept to sea behind them. Marcus rushed to the deck, desperately searching the ominous horizon for Theron's vessel. His stomach was churning, and it was growing harder to breathe. Suddenly they rose atop a wave and crashed hard against the breaking wharf. He saw another ship like his own in the distance. There on the deck he saw Theron. Another wave lifted them, and just before they fell from sight, Marcus made out Helghul next to her. Even through the dark storm, he imagined the triumphant smile on the Adversary's face.

Marcus was overcome with grief and concern, but by necessity his thoughts turned to survival. The ship was rocked by giant waves and slammed as if it would break apart. The winds had grown to hurricane force, and the immense land mass trembled and quaked violently. The ship needed to get away from the land or it would be broken against the rocks, and then he would never be able to protect Theron from Helghul.

A bright beacon had entered the atmosphere. A fiery ball had streaked across the sky, high above the clouds, imperceptible from Atitala. In the Northern Hemisphere, there was massive destruction as a meteor made impact, devastating the planet. The Earth's crust shifted and broke.

Fire had consumed Atitala, and only a few Atitalans still wailed, searching for a way to escape. The jewel-colored market tents and thatched rooves were no more, and the smell of sulfur and burned hair and skin was carried on the wind. There were visible dead everywhere—charred and defeated by their attempts to flee, they lay like driftwood in haphazard heaps at the edge of the fire.

The rain was lit by sparkling orbs hovering in the sky above. Marcus could see the spheres of light moving and beckoning and knew that they belonged to a higher consciousness, but he had no time to consider them now.

The sea lifted the boats, separating them and carrying them to distant horizons, while islands flooded and civilizations and landmasses were lost indefinitely. Cleaning, purging, destroying, the waves showed no mercy.

The entire world was in chaos, blanketed in choking dust that blocked the sun. Atitala creaked and groaned as it was battered and beaten. The land receded from the last boat. A deafening crack exploded from beneath—displaced by extreme pressure, the ground arched and lifted out of the water on the farthest southern shores. Molten rock glowed red and spewed miles into the air in an awesome show of natural power. Atitala lurched as the Earth's crust snapped under the strain and the northern coast was rocketed hundreds of yards into the punishing black sky. The descent began. Atitala slipped south, first slowly, then at a terrifying speed, displacing millions of gallons of seawater. The Emissaries watched, dumbfounded and devastated, as their homeland crested and the Grand Hall carved into the mountainside submerged before their eyes.

The boats would carry the grieving messengers to their destined shores. It was the dawn of a new Age.

Chapter 7

Love Lost

The Emissaries had been cast like seeds on the wind and would land where they were meant to be sown. While the others sought to comfort one another, Marcus isolated himself, alone with his worry for Theron. After three days, the dust thinned and the sun reappeared. Ten days later, Marcus's ship found land.

The thrill of seeing land in the distance was replaced by horror as they drew closer to shore. In the shallows, the debris became thicker: reed boats, bits of shelters, trees, and bodies—so many bodies. They were huge and bloated, greeting them with hollow stares. The arriving Emissaries were deeply disturbed by the hideous scene. Marcus watched desperately for signs of Theron's boat.

A former ally of Atitala, Stone-at-Center had been a most sacred site, an example of beauty and function. But now the land was hard to comprehend. Everything had been tossed, and it glistened with water and seaweed. Dead or dying fish, urchins, and all types of sea animals littered the ground. The homes were gone. The floods and earthquakes had wiped out millions of people—even some races and species entirely. Only a small number of people had survived. The only remaining structures were the interlocking walls cut in intricately connected H-shaped blocks, and the enormous 144-ton dock built from precisely honed slabs.

As the Emissaries of Atitala arrived, the cleanup and cremation of the decaying bodies and carcasses began. The Emissaries were in a state of constant prayer, and the ground and air around them vibrated with healing energy.

Marcus frantically disembarked, ignoring the disorder, the sadness, and the stench. He searched the arriving boats and questioned everyone he met. No one had seen Theron.

"Marcus, I need you here." Grey Elder beckoned from a nearby heap of rubble that had likely once been a temple or school. There were injured and helpless survivors everywhere.

"I haven't found any evidence of Theron. Are you perceiving anything?" Marcus asked, visibly upset. She was gone—his love, his soulmate. Helghul was with her, and she didn't know what he had become. Marcus hadn't warned her, and now he had no idea where she was or how to find her.

"There is much to do in rebuilding this sacred land. We need to work together," Grey Elder said, taking a few faltering steps. "Before all our knowledge is lost."

"I need to find Theron," Marcus said. "I need to know she's safe."

"The Emissaries will all arrive safely if it is meant to be so. You must accept your role here and leave Theron to hers."

"Helghul took her. He is something less than a man, Grey Elder. I should have told you sooner . . . I just couldn't speak of it," Marcus said.

"What is it you should have told me?"

"The night of the exodus, there was no time to tell anyone. I followed Helghul into the caverns sooner . . . I saw a ceremony.

Helghul was possessed by something powerfully evil that came up through the ground."

"Did you see anything else? Who else was there?" Grey Elder asked.

"There were other students and a cloaked man. I think it must have been Black Elder. I couldn't see his face. They killed the children . . . the missing children," Marcus said hoarsely. He gave in to the overwhelming urge to sob, and Grey Elder held him, leaning against the rock ledge behind him for support.

"Did you tell Theron? Does she know what Helghul has done?" Grey Elder asked.

"No," he croaked miserably. "There was no time."

"Marcus, there must be a reason that you witnessed the ceremony. We will have to wait and see how this unfolds."

"There was a memory potion that Helghul took," Marcus said, trailing off. "I took it too, but I don't know if there was enough; it was almost empty."

"Marcus, unfortunately you will suffer for this choice. It goes against the natural order to have memory in future lives," Grey Elder warned, closely reevaluating the young Emissary.

"I don't regret my choice," Marcus said defensively, sorry that he had witnessed the brutality but grateful for the memory potion.

"You have chosen a difficult path," Grey Elder said at last, and Marcus knew that it was true.

Chapter 8

The Search Begins

There were grueling days and months of work at Stone-at-Center—rebuilding wells, clearing debris, and tending to the bodies. Once the most pressing obligations were dispelled, Marcus became a traveler and spent days, weeks, and then years in search of Theron. As he searched, Marcus helped to reconstruct devastated villages in his path, but always he moved on at the first opportunity, determined to find his lost love.

A continent away, Theron searched every new face, year after year, hoping to be reunited with Marcus. The Emissaries in every region worked to rebuild. The Silver Age had come, but it, too, would descend, just as the Golden Age had. There was infrastructure to reestablish before consciousness and technology were completely forgotten by dying generations. Stories would be passed on orally until the Bronze Age, when it would no longer be possible for people to do so impeccably. Then, the Emissaries would rely on art, architecture, and written language to preserve the information.

Marcus never stayed in one place too long. He never failed to ask those he encountered if they had seen Theron. Had he known she was across the great ocean in Khem (later called Egypt) with Helghul and Red Elder, he would surely have commandeered a boat.

>❀< >❀< >❀<

Marcus's eyes grew poor, his knees gave him pain, and there were no proper healers to set him right, but still he walked and searched, sure that he would recognize Theron, even in old age. Marcus never found her.

Theron had missed him every day and wondered, until she died, where Marcus had ended up and if he had searched for her. He, too, always wondered if he might have just missed her—had she taken a left turn on a mountain pass when he had turned right? He never knew. Marcus found no peace and saw her around every corner, in every sinewy female figure and chestnut mop of hair. He heard her in every twinkling laugh. He would wake in the night, the feel of her hand in his, the smell of her skin, the image of her, so clear and vivid in his mind, and then the lucid dreams would dissipate, like smoke to the heavens. He could only be with her in his dreams.

The Emissary knew that when he died, he would be reborn into another shell, a new body, another lifetime. He prayed that in his next life, he would meet his love again and recognize her by her distinct karmic code, her glowing shine.

Marcus died at the age of 191, young for an Atitalan, but that world was gone, and as it was forgotten, so would be the days of great longevity. Marcus was remembered and celebrated by the people he had served, who had grown to care for him, in a small village in the Northern Hemisphere. He had never united with another. He had traveled north from Stone-at-Center over two continents to find Theron, and he had died alone when his weak body would allow him to search no more.

Chapter 9

The Burden of Memory

Atitala was long gone, cracked from its seat of strength. The tropical paradise had been submerged and now rested miles under the sea. The Earth, her terrain, and her people had been remade, and no continent had gone untouched.

The Emissaries had now reincarnated countless times. The wisdom and technological advancement of the Golden Age were lost and forgotten. As generations died and were reborn without memory, consciousness further descended into the Silver, Bronze, and Iron Ages of the Great Year Cycle. The evidence of former glory was buried and drowned. Many of the people had been reduced to living in caves, but they had made advancements over thousands of years and were rebuilding more sophisticated civilizations.

Marcus had guided them as best he could, but he alone remembered the way it had been in Atitala. Though he shared his knowledge, without tools, proof, or understanding, it was useless. It was like handing an infant an abacus. Even *he* did not now have the abilities he had once mastered. There was no telepathy; the lowered consciousness did not allow it. Only over time could people ascend to the level of understanding and former glory they had once known.

In each lifetime, Marcus's memories came back in pieces and, with them, feelings of loss. Childhood was a gift, free of past-life recollections, but his adolescent years were complicated and painful. By adulthood he regained vague memories, not only of Atitala, but of every lifetime since. He recalled people, places, and grief, and he was haunted throughout his lives by the appearance and disappearance of Theron. It was an inconsistent process. Sometimes the Emissary's Marcus-brain spoke to him clearly and the tiny threads wove a tapestry of who he was and all of the people he had been. But other times, in other incarnations, the memories would flood back like waves during times of stress, and the confusion and gravity of it all would make him question his own sanity.

Marcus was always able to read the shine of those around him and could easily recognize the Emissaries, who radiated in broad purple-and-violet energy regardless of their current bodies. They never knew him, not as Marcus nor as a fellow Emissary, but they were drawn to him. Sometimes it was like déjà vu, or a "Haven't we met?" experience, but their higher levels of consciousness helped them recognize one another as friends and allies.

Lifetime after lifetime, Marcus endured death: losing the people he had come to love, and remembering and missing them over and over again. Some he would see in future lives, a soul group with whom he had a significant connection, but he missed no one the way he missed Theron. Many lifetimes passed in which he failed to find her, where their destinies did not converge or they perhaps missed each other by hours, minutes, or seconds.

When they did come together in a lifetime, it seemed to Marcus that they were like actors in a theater. They were playing different roles, but there was always something strong and undeniable that pulled them together. Though she never knew him, never knew her true self, she was always Theron deep down. He knew her shine, which was as distinct as DNA—and seeing and feeling her filled him to his core. She felt him too, and when they were apart, neither was whole, though only *he* was tortured by it.

As Marcus continued as an Emissary, the loneliness and futility that he often felt wore him down. He berated himself for not doing more to expand the consciousness in each lifetime. He searched for Theron, incarnation after incarnation, only to discover the many forms their love would take and how many more ways he would learn to love.

Chapter 10

Synchronicity

Present day, Seattle, Washington

Everybody had shine. Quinn could see it all around him in the densely packed stadium. There were thousands of people surrounded in radiating bands of color. It was as clear as their breath on a cold day. He filtered through them, searching, one after another. People wore their colors like a cloak, and though most people were a warm mix somewhere in the middle, there were also extremes. Emissaries shone purple and indigo, and the Adversaries and dark souls were draped in shades of grey. Quinn avoided the murky ones. They were unpredictable and often reacted badly to his energy, though they never understood why. The light in him irritated them.

The Emissary preferred the nosebleed seats. He didn't care about football. He just wanted to see as many people as possible. Last week it had been an art gallery, Hempfest, and then a political rally. He feigned sociability when forced, but preferred observing from the outskirts, avoiding any attention and interaction that might distract him even for a minute. Quinn was looking for a particular indigo glow, and he didn't have time to waste on small talk. Theron was out there somewhere.

All these centuries later, Quinn remembered coupling with Theron in the Universal Grid—becoming soulmates. He had thought it was a guarantee that he would find her and be with her in every lifetime sooner . . . but it wasn't. It had proved to be far more complicated than that.

Quinn closed his coat against the rain as he walked back to his car from CenturyLink Field, keenly aware of each person who passed. Quinn had two abilities that he relied on: seeing shine, and deciphering the language of the universe through synchronicity. Shine was simple; synchronicity was a dance.

Swiss psychiatrist Carl Jung had coined the word *synchronicity* in the 1950s, but Marcus had been intimately acquainted with the concept since Atitala. It had been simple communication then, fully integrated and understood so that it did not need explaining. It was the knowing—a "meaningful coincidence" or a nudge in the right direction. It was the beautiful flow between seemingly unrelated events that was actually a source of guidance, a message of higher meaning, and Quinn knew that if he expanded his awareness, abating his doubt and skepticism, direction would come.

Understanding through synchronicity required Quinn to be an information seeker—alert, present, and in the moment at all times. He deciphered the signs like a mathematician would decode equations. In fact, he had been drawn to move to Seattle through synchronicity. This was where he was supposed to be. He had been considering Long Beach, Portland, or the Northwest, and it had come to crunch time. He'd given notice on his apartment, and month's end was nearing. Quinn had been no closer to a decision, but then he had tuned in to a series of synchronistic events that made the choice clear.

The Emissary had walked to his favorite coffee shop near his tiny apartment in the Soho neighborhood of New York City. It was full of old books, had torn leather stools, and a decrepit old counter that sold delicious European-style espresso.

"Closed. Starbucks coming soon," a sign on the door read. Quinn groaned, his head hanging. No warning, no goodbyes. It was just like life to pull away the little charms—to change.

"Hey, man," a soft voice behind him said with a nudge on his arm. A pretty Bohemian woman with a nose ring and a head wrap that bundled her thick dreadlocks held out a postcard to him. "Come see our show tonight. We're in town for a few days." She smiled. Her shine was pretty and light, but it wasn't Theron's. It was *never* Theron's.

Quinn looked at the card. She was a musician; *Seattle Underground* was the name of the band.

"You're from Seattle?"

"Yeah, we're touring all over," she said, then added thoughtfully, "This looks like a cool place."

"It was."

"Sorry about the Starbucks," she said.

"We can't blame everyone from Seattle for Starbucks," Quinn said, smiling.

"I know, right?" she said, suddenly aware of him, and interested.

He's handsome, she was thinking. *Funny, friendly, and cool. I might want to get to know him better.*

"I'm Shanti," she said.

"Quinn."

"I hope you come to the show. I think you'll like it."

"What kind of music do you play?"

"It's like, acoustic, conscious pop," she answered, as if it were the first time she had ever been asked.

"I'll try to make it," Quinn said, meaning it. It was just the kind of place he might find Theron. He tucked the flyer in his pocket, aware of the sexual attraction that had been awakened between them but indifferent to it. She was cute, and had great energy, but she wasn't his soulmate. Coupling with her would be pleasant, but sad at the same time. Experience had taught him that it was better to just move on, so Quinn had done so. He had said goodbye, and Shanti had continued down the street, promoting her gig and hoping to see the enigmatic man again.

Seattle . . . maybe it's meant to be Seattle, Quinn thought as he walked toward the next-best coffee joint. It was then that a sports headline caught his eye. The Seahawks had won the Super Bowl—Seattle again.

Throughout the rest of the day, *Seattle* had been shouted from websites, television and radio commercials, and random comments by strangers. Quinn's consciousness was aware and being directed. The Emissary's new home had been calling out to him. So Quinn had followed his instincts, leaving New York for the wide-open spaces of the Northwest . . . and for more relentless searching.

Chapter 11

The Work Continues

Present day, Seattle, Washington

There was a quick rap at the apartment door before it opened. Quinn looked up to see his pal. He had been in Seattle a few years, and though he hadn't found Theron, his buddy Nate helped ease his loneliness.

"Dude, you should lock your door!" Nate, a metrosexual artist in his late twenties, said as he let himself in. He wore skinny jeans, a long sloppy sweater, and a funky Bantu-knots hairdo that he was very proud of.

"If I had, you'd still be standing in the rain," Quinn pointed out, readjusting his robe.

"How goes the blog? You look like you're doing some pretty major research," Nate said, eyeing the pile of books and papers on the kitchen table as he helped himself to a cup of coffee. Quinn would have loved to tell Nate he was on a treasure hunt, looking for the fabled Emerald Tablet in order to keep it out of the hands of Helghul, but it was too unreal. There was no proof that the tablet or the Adversaries even existed. There was only his memory. There was a time, in the not-too-distant past, when revealing his knowledge and memories had seen him burned as a witch or locked away indefinitely. Quinn had learned to be cautious.

"How's it going with you?" Quinn asked instead, pushing back from his computer and rolling closer to the overstuffed chair behind him. Nate sat sideways. His long legs dangled over the worn arm as he drank.

"Not doing well, actually. My car's not driving for shit these days, and I hate the thought of taking the bus at my age. I really thought I was done with that, you know? Anyway, Sarah's been nagging like, insane, about the whole marriage-and-kids thing, and I was thinking, like seriously, if she's going to nag and bitch like this, do I really want to voluntarily get into some crazy, formal, man-made cage with her? Fuck no, so we had another huge fight. Hey, whatever happened with that woman who gave you her number at the Pearl Jam concert?" he asked, finally taking a breath.

Quinn passed him a joint and blew out a lungful of smoke. "Man, when someone asks how it's going . . . seriously, do you have to go into the unedited Bible-length version?" Quinn asked, shaking his head with a laugh.

"Yeah . . . explain *that*, why don't you? Why do people ask if they don't wanna know?"

"I want to know. Relax," Quinn said, amused by his friend's rant.

Nate was so easy to rile, but it was only because he cared so much. When Nate asked someone, "How's it going?" he meant it. He really wanted to know—right down to the smallest, most insignificant hangnail. If it mattered to you, Nate wanted to know. Quinn loved that about his buddy.

This wasn't their first lifetime together, and Quinn had been thrilled three years earlier when he and Nate had met on a small plane between Lake Arenal and Montezuma Beach in Costa Rica. They were the only two passengers on the tiny, turbulent flight, and they had been delighted to learn that they lived a mere ten miles apart back home in Washington State. Nate was shooting some second-unit film footage, and Quinn was searching for Theron. It was no coincidence they'd met. Though Nate did not have past-life memories, nor was he an Emissary, his aura was distinct, a fingerprint belonging only to him, and Quinn had recognized his spirit immediately.

"You didn't answer about that woman, the blonde. Did you call her?" Nate asked hopefully.

"Naw, I don't need the complications."

"You're practically a monk, dude," Nate teased, picking up the book next to him. *Tiwanaku Bolivia,* the cover said, but everything else was in Spanish, and Nate couldn't make it out. He shook his head, unable to share and interest in Quinn's dry and demanding literary choices. "You'd rather read this? She sounded chill, man . . . you don't have to marry her."

"Yeah, look who's talking," Quinn said, snorting.

Life was complicated enough. Relationships, especially romantic ones, never worked out for Marcus. There was only one Theron, and no matter who or where he was, no one else could reach that place within him. It was unfair to put other loving souls at such a disadvantage, and he had already endured so much pain.

Despite his best efforts, it wasn't easy to remain casual and aloof. In every lifetime, relationships were birthed and died. As the Ages declined and became denser, his connection to the higher collective consciousness had become more unclear, and the painful barbs of loss had attached to his heart.

Chapter 12

Mother Love

823 BCE, Stone-at-Center

Stone-at-Center was a most sacred site, a spiritual hub shrouded in ancient lore. Its energy was palpable, and the faithful from lands near and far made pilgrimages to its walls, its soil, and to pray in its temples. It was rumored that a visit there could cure the ill, soothe those in pain, and bring them closer to their gods.

Because of its religious significance and central location, the city was a key market and trading route. The area boasted an ancient pyramid and a monumental interlocking wall of precisely cut-and-laid stones, thought to have always been there. Curiously, there were many oceanic fossils unearthed, though the sea was many miles away. A stone boat, an example left to tell a story to future generations, lay mostly unnoticed. A greater power seemed to protect the sacred ground and preserve its ancient heritage. The prosperity and importance of the community made it a target of ambitious neighbors. Many times the great walled city had been attacked, and many times it had been successfully defended. It was built on miles of lush green plains. Traders and pilgrims approached from all sides, using the well-traveled llama caravan route to guide them. From the walls of the city, visitors were easily observed, and well-trained sentries thwarted invading armies.

For a thousand years, a noble family, believed by the populace to be chosen by the gods, ruled the sacred land, until one particularly cruel and cunning invader laid siege and fouled the succession. Marcus looked out on the vista as a dark procession neared. This was another lifetime, and many had passed. He had been many people and had lived many places since the first time he and the other Emissaries had landed at Stone-at-Center. He had been born and died as male and female and understood that the shell housing his soul was irrelevant. The spirit was eternal. Marcus was accustomed to his current female body. Looking down and seeing his hands so thin and delicate, so much like Theron's hands, they sparked him to remember.

His life as Sartaña, the High Priestess of Stone-at-Center, had been rewarding. He was a spiritual leader and healer, and though he had not met Theron in this incarnation, he had experienced the miracle of carrying and birthing a child. He felt the love and concern of a mother for her offspring and was grateful for it.

Sartaña did not remember everything. Whether it was because Marcus had only sipped the remnants of a discarded memory potion, or because that was the nature of the elixir, she did not know. Her past lives were like hazy dream recollections, bits and pieces of pictures torn up and scattered, which she painstakingly tried to reassemble with the unpredictable assistance of her Marcus-brain.

The land she looked upon had changed considerably. The ocean that had, centuries before, carried Marcus to these same shores had subsided and was now miles away. The lush huarango tree line had receded as the population and consumption had increased, and the soil had become dry and dusty.

The priestess prepared herself, waiting in dread, knowing that her warriors had been defeated. She was gazing across the Altiplano from the higher ground of the palace as the people rushed between dwellings. The elderly left their outdoor perches for the safety of their huts. Fires were left to burn out. The women rushed about, urging their children and animals indoors, concealed from the conquering army. There were no middle-aged men; only the very old and young remained. Everyone else had been called to the city's defense. Word had come ten minutes earlier, by way of a frantic messenger, that the resistance had been crushed and a vicious conqueror was on his way.

Sartaña could see the progression approaching from her window. She ignored her muddled Marcus-brain to concentrate on the task ahead. She must prepare her people—especially her son, Amaru—for whatever would come.

Be brave! she told herself after a brief meditation. The priestess did not want to increase the fear already vibrating through the palace and village. She had to focus harder to hide the tremors in her hands. She released the terror knotting in her throat through deep breaths. Sartaña had to appear confident, regal, and strong.

Sartaña turned from her chamber window, her fists tightly clenched as if the pressure in her hands could subdue the angst in her heart. She was dressed in traditional regal robes of finely woven cloth dyed deep pink, orange, and blue. The hem of her long cape told the story of her people and had been stitched intricately with gold thread, symbols, and designs. Servants helped place a fine gold-and-feather headdress on her dark hair, which by its very weight and nature made her appear majestic and proud. As she reached the door, her son was brought to her.

Amaru was ten years old and tall for his age. His dark eyes telegraphed his fear as he ran to his mother's waiting embrace. The top of his head just reached her chin, and she bent to greet him, eye to eye, skillfully keeping her heavy headdress in balance.

"My son, our enemies approach," she said, embracing him tightly. She felt his fear and confusion and drank in the smell of the dust in his hair and the fresh air on his skin.

Center yourself, Sartaña thought. Little ribs, arms, and precious hands clung to her. This moment—the now—with her son folded in her arms, was heavenly, and she knew it would end too soon. Her Marcus-brain was firing, and her synapses sent messages, warning of the hardships to come.

"No one will tell me anything. What's happened? Is it Father?" Amaru complained. He was terrified, and reaching out, he soothed himself as he had often done as a toddler, finger-tracing the flower-shaped scar that was branded into his mother's upper arm.

Sartaña remembered how her son used to run his tiny fingers over the raised white skin and ask her repeatedly if it hurt. He loved the story of her coming-of-age ceremony, when she had been honored with the symbol of the Seed of Life: six circles coming together, within a seventh that looked like a flower.

"I've had no word, but it cannot be good."

"Is he dead?"

"I fear it is so," she said, faltering as her son responded to the news tearfully. "I need you to be strong. I must welcome our new leader and pray that there is no more bloodshed," Sartaña said seriously. The priestess lifted her son's drooping, tear-streaked face to her own, longing to ease the alarm and sorrow in his dark eyes. She used the edge of her precious robe and wiped his cheeks and nose dry.

"What will happen now?" the boy asked, sniffling and wiping away his tears, wanting to behave bravely, as a young man and future leader should.

"This is a dangerous time. If we are to survive, we must submit to our conquerors. The citizens must accept this new order." Her face was lined with concern and desperation. She had no time to feel anguish for her own loss. Her only concern was to save her son and protect her people.

"Will they kill us?" Amaru asked, his stomach turning and contracting involuntarily.

"I do not know. We must be cautious. Our adversary must not see you as a threat. It is not safe to leave now; all the gates are breached. I am going to send you away. You will live in a nearby village with the family of my servant, Malaya. You must not return here. You must not tell anyone who you are. They will protect you and say you are the son of a farmer, an orphan. She will take you now and hide you in the city until it is safe to leave. Do you understand?" Sartaña demanded, holding her son's shoulders and searching his face for comprehension.

Amaru understood completely. His father, the High Priest and leader of these vast lands, had schooled him since the age of five. He had been taught the ways of his people—farming, politics, spirituality, and defense. Amaru knew that as an heir to the throne, he would be eliminated by the conquering leader.

Sartaña's servant, Malaya, entered and gave the boy a bundle of worn clothing and sandals more suited to a peasant child. She handed the High Priestess a small bowl. Sartaña dipped her fingers into the bowl and, while saying a prayer aloud, used the soil within to camouflage the cheeks and arms of her son. It served as both a blessing and a disguise. "You must change and go now, with Malaya. I will see you again someday. Do not seek me out. I will come for you. I will send word when I can. Promise me, Amaru. Try to blend in. Do not bring trouble down upon these good people who help us."

"But when will I see you? How long?" he asked, his youth and vulnerability plain. Amaru realized that he was leaving all that he knew and that he might never see his mother again. He began to cry, and fresh tears streaked the dirt and grime meant to help him appear more common.

"I don't know. To know that you are safe is all I ask. Now go, and do not be seen! We can no longer be sure who to trust," she said to Malaya as well as her son. "You must hurry, for time is short. Know that I love you and carry you with me always." She touched her hand to her heart. Sartaña hid her own misery so that she would not upset him further. Amaru's tears fell in dark water stains onto her dress, despite his wish to be brave and suppress them.

Marcus ached to be saying goodbye. The love that he felt, this mother love, was like nothing he had ever experienced. The reality of having the most precious and vulnerable part of himself walking outside his body was overwhelming. It compared to the love he still felt for Theron but, in this lifetime, overshadowed it. The child was a miracle from Sartaña's own body—from her very flesh—and a child brought a helplessness and dependence that a lover did not. Theron was like fleeting smoke, but Amaru was present, real, and in jeopardy.

Marcus's losses were now so many. For each one in this lifetime, there were a hundred more already survived, remembered—burdens casting their shadows on his heart. War was nothing new, and death and loss were a part of every life he had lived.

Amaru was courageously shuttled away by Malaya, and Sartaña left her chamber. Flanked by her personal servants, she passed through the palace's multicolored rooms to the outdoor courtyard. She struggled to quiet the nervous tremors that shook her hands and legs, and she was glad that she had not eaten anything, certain that she would vomit if she had. She was conscious that she must appear calm and composed to reassure her people and to face whatever might come.

Sartaña walked directly to the two beautifully carved, massive stone thrones that rested in the center of the courtyard at the top of a stairway. Behind her, an ancient arched gateway to the sun framed the scene and added to the spectacle of her beauty and courage. She took her seat and was painfully aware that the empty chair next to her would never again be rightly filled. Her grief assaulted her once again and mingled with the knowledge that she would very likely meet a cruel fate herself very soon. She continued to pray silently for Amaru, desperate that he should escape the wrath of the coming conqueror.

Sartaña waited. There was nothing else she could do. The sun moved overhead, warming her and causing beads of sweat to rise on her brow beneath the heavy diadem and prickling her spine.

Finally, a distant rumble grew to a roar as the conquering multitude passed the unprotected gates into the sacred city. Warrior after warrior marched, talked, laughed, and cheered as they followed their exultant leader to the central courtyard—a seemingly endless trail shrouded in a cloud of dust. The stench of sweat and blood filled the path walkways; the air was thick with their unfamiliar odors.

The citizens huddled in their huts, shaking with grief and fear. Some peeked curiously at the awful procession, instantly terrified by the spectacle of spears and blood-soaked posts with the severed heads of their men stacked three and four high symbolizing the "taking" of their identity. Fathers, grandfathers, and friends all reduced to body parts and trophies and paraded ghoulishly through the familiar lanes.

The leader, Katari, climbed the stone steps unchecked, flanked by his personal guards, the Puma-warriors. Each of the elite soldiers wore a dramatic mask or headdress meant to terrify and intimidate their rivals. In his hand, dangling from his spear, Katari raised the severed head of the conquered High Priest: staring in frozen shock, and still wet with fresh blood. Sartaña stared in horror at her mate's head swinging and bouncing with each step. His kind lips and laughing eyes were distorted and ruined. The grotesque object looked surreal, and her brain could hardly comprehend it. Katari ignored the dried blood on his skin; his thick flat forehead and wide nose were in direct contrast to the fine features of his victim.

The war was lost, and the rewards were yet to be claimed by the victors. Sartaña, sitting erect and proud, concealed the fear bubbling up inside of her as she clutched the cold stone arms of her throne, her knuckles white and tense.

I have seen this before, she thought inwardly, staring at her captor. *I've seen* him *before!* An icy hatred filled her as the sinister Katari approached. His face became familiar somehow. Suddenly Sartaña was filled with overwhelming panic as her Marcus-brain recognized the karmic code through the grime, the paint, and the blood; saw the black, cruel shine emanating in all directions and leeching into the very ground at Katari's feet. His dark life force had been visible to her from a great distance but had been indistinct. Now he was near enough and focused on her so that she recognized him completely. Her unconscious intuition screamed at her in alarm, and she acknowledged the pure hatred in his eyes.

Helghul! She felt panicked. She didn't have full recall. She searched her memories, striving to understand. Her Marcus-brain was scorched by the sight and feel of him, and her recollections struck her like lightning bolts.

The conquering foreigner stopped in front of Sartaña, and he and the priestess met face-to-face for the first time. Not trusting her legs to hold her, she remained rooted to her seat as she wondered, *What will he do? Will he murder me here?*

Sartaña felt the heat of his foul breath on her skin, and the urge to kill him swelled within her. It was a dark impulse. She looked from the dagger at his waist to his spear, where her husband's head hung, and the priestess wondered bitterly how his death could be accomplished.

Endless gruesome scenarios had played over in her head in the mere seconds it took for the brute to speak. He bent forward, his face only inches from hers.

"You do not rise to greet your new king . . . Marcus?" Katari hissed in a low growl audible only to her. Sartaña was startled by the use of her spirit-name, and her mind was reeling. Her ancient Marcus-consciousness spoke to her then, more loudly than before.

Helghul, she heard again in her head. In Katari's eyes, Helghul's energy was stronger and more evil than ever. The Adversary had learned a great deal since his days in Atitala.

"Helghul?" Sartaña said under her breath. Her response unwittingly informed Katari that she, too, had memory. The warrior was startled by the unexpected recognition, and the Beast within him immediately transmitted inside his head.

This Emissary is dangerous! This one is not like the others! the Beast warned.

Katari was troubled that Marcus had memory. He regrouped quickly and masked his concern with a scowl, displaying his jagged, filthy teeth. He stepped back and thrust his gruesome spear forward, dangling the monstrous head next to her face, taunting her. Sartaña closed her eyes and shuddered involuntarily.

Laughing, Katari turned to address his Puma-warriors and the villagers, who had begun meekly emerging to witness the inevitable transition of power. He raised his hands high in the air, still holding his spear, and effortlessly summoned silence. He walked to a nearby stone, only slightly shorter and wider than he was. It had a thick, perfectly honed hole all the way through, into which he spoke. His voice was amplified to every corner.

"Hear me, citizens . . . you see your master is my plaything; your warriors are no more. I, Katari, claim this land, these people, and all within its bounds. My Puma-warriors will garner the spoils of war and choose homes and wives among you. There need be no more bloodshed. Your daughters and the elders may stay, but your sons will fend for themselves.

"No warrior here will raise the boy of another man, only to have him slit his throat in his sleep someday. Women, do not think that you will take your children and run; it will not be permitted. Those who attempt to leave or to resist will die a cruel and painful death, as others have before them. Any male child within the city walls by sundown will be executed," he commanded.

"Priestess, you may address your people. Choose your words wisely," Katari said, turning to her. She understood and proudly rose to speak to her people, most of whom had now come out of their dwellings and were in a state of extreme distress.

Sartaña moved in front of the speaking stone. "My people, good citizens, the battle is over, and we have come to this wretched end. It is time now to save your children, to save our city, and to accept our fate. Our protectors have been defeated. Let the violence end today. Bundle your sons; put them in the care of the capable older boys. We pray that the Great Spirit will protect them and carry them to the bosom of a sympathetic neighbor," she called out, strong and steady in her urgings and seething silent hatred in her belly.

Suddenly, a quick movement to her left drew her eye, and in an instant, her calm dissolved. "Amaru, *no!*" she cried, lunging too late.

In seconds, the ten-year-old boy was cut down by an assault of spears from Katari's guard. The macabre head of his father, still in the murderer's grasp, jiggled and jerked in protest of the death of his would-be avenger and only son.

Sartaña screamed and ran to her child where he had fallen, three spears perpendicular to his crumpled body cutting deep into his young flesh. Her headdress of yellow-and-purple feathers clattered noisily to the ground behind her, its fine gold bent and ruined. Thick, bloody strands of her hair were torn out by the weight of it and lay in the twisted mess.

"Amaru!" she cried out, crawling under her son's bleeding frame and pulling him into her lap as though she were cradling a newborn.

The boy was unable to speak or to focus, his eyes were wild with fear, and high-pitched squeals of agony escaped him. A small sword, not even a man-sized weapon, fell useless from his prepubescent hand to the dirt beside them. He writhed and twisted, pulling his right leg up to his belly; his left leg, obviously ignoring commands from his brain, remained limp and bent awkwardly in the dust. The wooden pillars protruding from his soft, young flesh swung and jerked as he moved, hitting against his mother as she frantically placed one hand to his cheek, trying to ease his suffering. Her other hand was pressed across his body to steady him against her and stop the flesh of his wounds being torn further by the protruding rods.

Tears poured from Sartaña's eyes as she moaned inconsolably. Her Marcus-brain was reeling and had no voice at all. In this dire moment, there was no higher brain, no time for enlightened thinking; there was only survival and instinct. There was only the love of a mother and her child, a love bond superior to and stronger than all others.

Suddenly Amaru's writhing and howls ceased. His silence was worse. He went limp in her arms, his young eyes staring, frozen in surprise, as his spirit was released. She fell, useless against her grief, and collapsed in anguish. In that moment, she longed to die. Life was too cruel, too sad, and not worth living at all; first her mate and now her son. In the time it had taken the sun to cross the sky, her world had completely unraveled.

Sartaña prayed to join her son in death and was too overwhelmed to entertain the anger that tried to take hold of her. Her Marcus-voice broke through, reminding her that Amaru's soul was safe and well, and that her people needed her guidance, but she couldn't listen. The greatest part of her lay murdered in the dirt. Her pain was blinding and unbearable.

Mercilessly, Katari bent behind her and whispered in her ear, "The fool merely saved me the effort of the hunt."

Without a second thought, a howling Sartaña raked her fingernails across the stubbly cheek unwisely close to hers. Katari jumped back, clubbing Sartaña in the face with the blunt end of his spear. The blow jolted her and sent blinding white sparks to the center of her brain. She splayed on her side, unconscious beneath the corpse of her boy. At least for the time being, there was peace and respite from her pain.

Katari ordered them removed, wiping his stinging, bloody cheek with the back of his hand; his Helghul-brain was fuming at her impudence, and the Beast was demanding retribution. The Adversary's hatred for Marcus was further ignited and burned profoundly. At that moment, he began formulating his plan for how to best use his fellow Atitalan to his utmost benefit.

Helghul wondered about this reunion. *What synchronicity and meaning does it have for me? What purpose does it serve?* He was pleased but not surprised to have discovered Marcus in that place of spiritual importance—it was certain to be inhabited by an Emissary. Katari had chosen this key energy point for that very reason. In Khem, hundreds of lifetimes before, Red Elder had said that the Emissaries would rebuild the sacred sites. He had searched them out, hoping to find the Emerald Tablet; however, the treasured item had still not been found.

Marcus and Helghul had not crossed paths since the night of the exodus, though he had longed for this moment. He remembered gleefully watching Marcus ashore, whipped by the violent storm, frantically running and calling to Theron. He could still feel the triumph he had experienced as she had struggled against him and was prevented from joining her unworthy lover.

Helghul had met many Emissaries in past lives, and he had recognized and manipulated them easily. He worked ruthlessly toward his own purpose: to further the darkness and add doubt and fear to the world of humans; and to create chaos, to rule, and to dominate, dividing the people from one another and crushing the hopeful, positive energy of his fellow Atitalans.

Marcus having memory and recognizing him had been a surprise. Who would have given Marcus the memory potion? Certainly not White Elder. It was an act of defiance unexpected of an Emissary. The new revelation changed things for Helghul and made Marcus a more formidable enemy than the other Atitalans. Marcus could be a danger to him, with his past-life memory and higher understanding.

Katari wondered if Marcus might have information about the Emerald Tablet. Is that why he had memory? Was he set apart from the other Emissaries, some sort of protector? Sartaña must be carefully dealt with.

The Beast compelled Katari to murder the priestess and eliminate Marcus, but Katari had many reasons for keeping the Emissary alive, apart from his aspiration of finding the Emerald Tablet. Katari knew that Sartaña might be useful in manipulating the locals, and he did not want to take a chance that Marcus could be reborn and possibly have the upper hand against him. Murdering the Emissary would be emotional and unwise, so Katari, resisting the pressure of the bloodthirsty Beast, decided to keep his foe captive and under his control.

The Bronze Age of the Great Year Cycle was winding down into the Iron Age. Stone-at-Center was immersed in a time of tyranny and servitude such as it had never known, and Helghul's energy was gaining influence and power by the year.

Katari immediately settled into the palace. The rotting, severed head of the High Priest was still attached to the new leader's spear, which leaned carelessly disregarded in the corner of the very room where the deceased had once lived and loved in life. It was soon to be baked, smoked, and shrunken, eventually to be worn as a trophy on Katari's grisly belt.

Katari's brutal Puma-warriors had performed as commanded and now rested, rewarded with their new shelters and their women. Publicly murdering the High Priest's heir in such a ruthless manner had ensured the maximum cooperation of the citizens and had eliminated Amaru as a future threat. Fear was a powerful tool, one that Katari encouraged and used readily, along with material reward, of course.

The male children had been expelled to fend for themselves, with little more than water bladders to sustain them. Even the very youngest infants were ordered out and were swaddled and tied to the backs of the older children. Terrified and confused, the parade of young boys, many crying and begging their mothers to allow them to stay, was marched away at the point of a spear. Toddlers wailed and screeched, dragged by the older boys, whose parents had warned them in no uncertain terms what would happen if they disobeyed.

"I'll be good, Mama."

"Please, Mama," so many little voices rang out, "let me stay."

"Why can't you come?" the voices wailed, but on and on they moved, bewildered and lost before they were even outside the walls.

More than one young mother was unable to bear the parting and chose to take her own life and that of her children rather than send them to certain death outside the gates. Their huts were emptied, and they were burned without ceremony, without prayer, without respect.

Women continued to disappear in the weeks following the expulsion of the boys, searching for their lost children. Most of them were dragged back to the city in varying states of hopelessness, hysteria, and injury without their children in tow. They were punished publicly as an example to deter others.

A dark, heavy pall blanketed the region. The devastated citizens sadly accepted their new High Priest and self-pronounced king and were as helplessly divided as the spoils of war.

Despite his disdain for Marcus, Katari was a cunning and strategic leader who clearly understood Sartaña's influence. She was born of a highly revered family and was believed to have been ordained by the gods. The people were devout, and Katari intended to use her influence to control them. As he plotted, his plans for Sartaña reached beyond her role as the High Priestess.

Two days after the death of Sartaña's son, Katari sent an order for her to appear before him. He reclined nonchalantly, cracking a peanut and popping its meat into his mouth. The shell fell to the floor, adding to the heap already there. His breastplate and thin beard were littered with crumbs and casings, and he breathed loudly as he chewed. The ruler looked up from his food as Sartaña entered the large royal-blue chamber, formerly her husband's private room. She still wore the bloodstained dress she had been wearing days before, and she was gripped on either side by a guard. Her hands were bound tightly in front of her, and a large bruise had swelled on her cheek where the butt of Katari's spear had struck her. Though her eyes were puffy from crying, there was no sign of tears as she stared hatefully at her captor.

As she entered, an unpleasant odor of rot mingled with body odor and smoke assaulted her immediately, and she wrinkled her nose in disgust. It was so unlike the scent of copal incense that used to draw her in. It was the first time she had been there since the invasion, and it pained her to see this pig of a man lounging so disrespectfully and intimately in her mate's space. She noticed the head so casually overlooked: rotting, stinking. She forced herself to look away. She was determined not to cry in front of Katari, but for a moment, a wave of nausea twisted her belly, constricting her throat, causing her mouth to water.

She turned her gaze toward the opposite side of the room where the bedroll lay, soft and inviting, a place where she had found so much pleasure and tenderness in times past.

Katari studied her as she adjusted to the scene. Even in her grief, Sartaña was striking to look at. Her eyes shone, and her mouth was full and sensuous. Her thick, luxurious hair hung to her narrow waist in loose dark curls, concealing the missing patches that the headdress had torn from her scalp. Katari let her wait while he dropped more discarded shells and chewed noisily.

Sartaña studied him, trying to reconcile the memories of Helghul that had been flashing back to her constantly over the past two days. Clearly there was something Marcus wanted to convey to her. Helghul's dark, prickly nature was obvious, and he repulsed and offended her in every way—even without warning from her higher self. He had murdered her husband and her son and had conquered her city; it was obvious he was a Beast. Why had they been brought together?

Katari's energy made her shudder involuntarily. He felt her hatred and enjoyed it. He stood and walked around her, looking her up and down lasciviously. He stopped directly in front of her and finally spoke.

"Nice breasts, Marcus," he taunted, reaching out and roughly grabbing her through her blood-encrusted dress. Bits of nuts flew out of his mouth as he spoke, and Sartaña stepped away from him, unable to use her hands. She had dreaded this.

Katari made eye contact with her for the first time, and a sharp pain shot through her skull to a bulging gland throbbing behind her eyes. The discomfort was hers alone, and he smirked at her, seemingly unaffected. He grabbed the hair at the nape of her neck and wrenched her head back as he spoke menacingly into her ear. "I intend to take you as a wife. I want a child, a son to unite the people." Sartaña winced painfully at the word *son*.

"You disgust me! I will die before I let you touch me!" she snarled through clenched teeth, hoping to provoke him, hoping he would end her misery on the spot. Sartaña looked strong and defiant, her jaw jerked forward and her eyes on fire. But the truth of it was that she was exhausted, beaten down by the death of her mate and her son and her inability to help her people. She had entirely lost the will to live.

"You are weak, as you always were! A cruel, unloved dark soul!" she goaded. Katari slapped her hard—once, twice, blow after blow. Sartaña begged for death, trying to manipulate him into releasing her, and would not be silenced. She was knocked to the floor, but her diatribe continued. "I saw the hideous ten-headed entity that entered you! He is your master! You're a pawn, used by darker souls! You're a fool," she continued, Marcus urging her on, certain that if she continued, Helghul would murder her, releasing her anguished soul to the universe.

Helghul was stunned by her venomous words. *She knew!* Marcus knew about the Beast, and had witnessed the ceremony! *But how?*

Enraged by Sartaña's relentless curses, Katari wanted to silence her but refused to strike a fatal blow. He was determined that she would bear his child; he would control her.

"You will die when I decide!" Katari shouted, controlling his anger. He nodded to the guards, and they released her, taking a step back. "I like to know exactly where your spirit resides; it eliminates any chance of surprises." Marcus understood that Helghul saw him as a threat. "You will bear me a son. He will be a king accepted by the people, and he will be wise and cunning like me . . . nothing like your foolish boy, so easily destroyed."

Sartaña threw herself on him, her bound hands working together feebly to strike blows. Katari easily pushed her off, and she crashed to the floor, unable to break her fall.

The guards hauled her up painfully, and she cried out against their grip and against Katari, spewing more repugnance at him. He approached her now, the guards easily constricting her struggling frame.

"Oh, the hopelessness, the despair!" Katari gloated, holding her chin tightly in his coarse hand, his foul breath only inches from her nose. Then, dropping his voice, he added, "I feel your despair, Sartaña. You reek of it! I taste it, and it arouses me. Have you considered it . . . killing yourself?"

"Never!" she said defiantly. Marcus knew that suicide was not an option. It brought disharmony in the afterlife, and he would never find Theron if he was stuck in limbo, his energy trapped in the world between.

"Your suffering has only just begun," Katari warned, and in one motion, he grabbed the collar of her dress and tore it down the front, exposing her breasts. The guards were fiendishly excited by the show and held her more cruelly, twisting her arms over her head. Katari directed the guards to turn her around, not wanting to look into her eyes. He lowered his trousers to his thighs and lifted the shredded garment still covering her. Excited by his power over her, he then entered her violently from behind, tearing her tender skin.

Katari pushed her away when he was through. She stumbled, and the Puma-warriors grabbed her by both arms. Her robe gaped without her hands to secure it, and they returned her to a secured room on the far side of the palace.

Sartaña had screamed and struggled that first time Katari had forced himself on her, but she quickly realized that the fight excited him. Regardless of how much she resisted, he would injure but not kill her, though she wished he would. In the weeks and months that followed, Katari came to the small, plain chamber where she was imprisoned many times. She chose to lay limp and lifeless, though he struck her and goaded her mercilessly to try to elicit a response from her. He bombarded her with cruel comments about her dead son and husband, but she refused to be baited. Her courage and self-control enraged him, and he was often unable to maintain an erection.

No matter what she did, he beat her. Sartaña's inner Marcus-brain warned her of Helghul's darkness, and showed distressing images of a ten-headed beast seeping from the ground—snarling, and gnashing its fangs. The same inner voice attempted to console her, promising that Amaru's spirit was safe and out of pain, but she was plagued by the memories of his murder and grieved for him terribly. Sartaña felt useless. She had been unable to protect her people, her husband, and her son from Katari, and her mind was full of information and visions that made no sense.

Sartaña's ancient awareness needled her. She was confused by memories of Atitala, a time when there was no darkness, and they made returning to her present suffering and uncertainty more torturous.

Sartaña's menses stopped by the second moon cycle of her captivity, and soon her belly became round. At first she was distraught, wondering if the child would be a demon like the father. Would she give birth to a dark soul sent only to cause pain in the world?

Her concerns disappeared with the first movement of the fetus inside her. A baby was a miracle, and Sartaña was filled with the wonder of the soul inside her. Marcus was awed once again to know a mother's heart and feel the overwhelming love and selflessness.

Unhappy to give Katari what he most desired, but grateful to end the cycle of rape and abuse, Sartaña announced her pregnancy to the wretched king. Katari halted his cruel attacks on Sartaña. He was determined that she have a healthy child, so she was brought food and fruit and wine to comfort her as the baby grew. Her cold straw mat was replaced with a soft bedroll, and though she was always guarded and isolated, she rested comfortably in her humble room. She began to wonder if her Marcus-memories were simply dreams. Perhaps Katari's most evil days were behind him. She became hopeful for her unborn child.

The flow of pilgrims and traders to Stone-at-Center had slowed since news of the violent takeover had spread. As a result, the prosperity of the city had waned significantly. Katari realized he must reestablish the confidence of those in the surrounding lands if he wished his kingdom to return to its former prosperity and stature. He began to parade Sartaña in public as the High Priestess, but he never spoke to her except for the occasional harsh remark. Sartaña complied willingly, more concerned for the child in her belly than for herself.

The pregnancy was difficult; the fetus was never at rest and rolled, turned, and kicked relentlessly. Her labor started without warning, and in less than two hours, with the help of a midwife, a slick, healthy baby boy slid painfully into the world. The child was easily soothed at his mother's breast. Sartaña held his tiny hands and stared into his face as he suckled and slept. He briefly opened his squinting eyes to the newness of the world, and she wept uncontrollably for the love of her new son, coupled with grief for the one murdered before him.

Inti was a happy infant and made it easy for them to bond. Sartaña held him and sang to him for hours. Mother and child spent every day together, and their special relationship grew as time passed. Yet Sartaña lived in constant fear that at any moment, her son would be taken from her.

The city and surrounding areas, desperate for good news, rejoiced at the announcement of the birth, and a carefully calculated celebration of one hundred days ensued. Determined to restore prosperity to the region, Katari hosted highly visible ceremonies, extravagant feasts, and spectacles on the terraces of the Akapana Pyramid. The downtrodden citizens were easily manipulated, and they warmed to their new High Priest when he joyfully presented his new son and heir, Inti. Katari insisted that Sartaña sit at his side, smiling, and nodding regally to the people. She was determined to make no more trouble for Katari. She wanted only to protect and teach their son as much as possible.

Within months of Inti's birth, Sartaña found herself wondering at the spirit that had been born to her. This child was so familiar, touched her so deeply, that she ached at the briefest parting. Sartaña kept Inti with her always; he was typically slung across her body in a fold of finely painted fabric. The boy never cried except when parted from his mother. He radiated light and goodness to everyone he met. Sometimes in the quiet moments of the day, she would see visions of him as someone else—a woman, vibrant and shimmering, but always so dear to her, so familiar and good. Then one day she saw it: her Marcus-brain recognized the indigo shine of Theron. She realized then that her past dreams were true memories, and they flooded to her in ever-clearer waves.

Sartaña knew it was inevitable that Helghul would also recognize Theron's karmic code. It was energy completely the opposite of his own darkness. Most likely Katari had already recognized Theron's spirit, though he continued to show little interest in Inti, other than at public events. The busy leader generally left the pair alone, consumed by his role as the High Priest and plotting further conquests to the north and south.

As Inti grew, he spent many hours in Sartaña's humble chamber playing, singing, and telling stories. Early in life he proved himself an extraordinary child. He began walking very young and showed a remarkable ability for language and reason. Sartaña educated him in mathematics, the healing arts, the science of the stars, and spirituality. She recited her imprecise memorization of the Emerald Tablet and taught him the nature of the universe and oneness. The universal truth was clear to Marcus, as it was for the other Emissaries, though loneliness and isolation remained a confusing aspect of the human condition.

Often, while Sartaña was weaving, Inti would climb into her lap and take her face in his pudgy toddler hands, bringing his forehead to hers. He would sit there, remaining still, unlike children of his age, and she would feel Theron's energy flowing through him.

Four years had passed since Inti's birth, and Sartaña had been permitted to resume her work as a spiritual guide and healer to her people, communing with nature's elements and maintaining the balance of natural and human forces necessary for cosmic well-being. She had cultivated a garden of useful plants and herbs at the southern tip of the palace walls, and she and Inti spent hours there together telling stories, laughing, and learning from each other. She taught him how to speak to the seeds and to sow them with his hands and feet in the soil.

One day Sartaña sat against the shaded stone wall taking a break from the heat. Inti leaned against her, and they shared a pear as he traced the scarred ridges of the seed of life on Sartaña's upper arm, just as Amaru used to do.

"Does it hurt?" Inti asked, not for the first time. He was always fascinated by the symbol.

"No," she said, smiling. "It's an honor to display the symbol of eternal life and unity. It is the mark of how we are all connected. We are all one," she explained. It was an exchange they'd had many times, but this time Inti's four-year-old mind posed a new, more challenging question.

"Was Papa chosen by God?" he asked.

Sartaña paused, unsure how to answer. Was Katari chosen by God? Helghul? For every positive there is a negative, for every yin, a yang. Her Marcus-brain contemplated the question, and Sartaña considered her answer carefully.

"It is complicated, Inti," she finally answered, kissing his rumpled black hair and pulling him close.

Theron's energy grew stronger and more obvious every day. Though it filled Sartaña with a complete love and connection that she adored, she worried that Katari would take him away, that Helghul would tear them apart once again.

Near the end of Inti's fifth year, as Sartaña had feared and expected, Katari began to take a greater interest in him. He had recognized Theron, just as Sartaña had, but Katari exhibited no resentment toward his unrequited love. Inti began spending more time learning at his father's side, severely limiting his time with his mother. As a result, the child's behavior became more demanding, rude, and entitled.

Katari was more fond of the clever boy than he would admit, and enjoyed him as a companion and a student. Inti wished to please his father, but he felt frightened and intimidated by him. Also, he missed Sartaña.

Inti's fifth birthday was approaching, which, according to local customs, signaled a formal transfer from the care of his mother into his father's hands for instruction. Sartaña had explained to Inti that he would be seeing her progressively less in the days and months to come. Her intuition warned her that Katari would separate them more than was typical, and she was preparing him for that eventuality.

Next to the palace, with its multicolored rooms decorated in deep royal blue, emerald green, neon orange, and fluorescent pinkish-red, rose a step pyramid six terraces high that overlooked the Altiplano, the palace, and the courtyard. Atop the pyramid fortress, Sartaña sat with Inti on the edge of one of many reflective pools. Inti sat on the stone ledge staring at their reflections in the shallow pool. Though Sartaña could clearly see Theron's indigo shine playfully swirling around her son and mixing with her own Marcus energy, when she looked into the water, they were gone.

"When I am High Priest, I will make these pools deeper so I can lie in them," Inti told his mother as he swirled the water with his chubby finger, rippling their image.

"The pools are for learning," Sartaña told him.

"What am I to learn from water?" Inti asked, wiping his wet finger on his pants. His self-importance was growing, and Sartaña knew that keeping him from becoming arrogant and counteracting Katari's influence would be difficult.

"Look into the pool. What do you see?" Sartaña asked.

"Me and you."

"And what else?" his mother prompted.

"I see the sky and the sun and . . . there's the moon!" Inti exclaimed, noticing the pale white half-moon. He had not noticed it earlier, and he liked seeing the moon in the daytime. He looked at the sky to confirm that it was indeed there.

"That's right. As above, so it is below," Sartaña said, repeating the words of the Emerald Tablet. She pointed up, then at herself and Inti. "We are reflections of the heavens."

"When I die, will I see you in the heavens, Mama?" Inti asked, still staring at his mother's face in the pool.

"It is certain," Sartaña promised. Standing to leave, Inti stood beside her, wrapping his arms around her legs and burying his face in the folds of her dress. His head barely reached her hip, and she hugged him to her, her heart full, and aching with the knowledge that their time together was in Katari's cruel hands.

"I will miss you," Sartaña whispered.

"Where are you going?" Inti asked in alarm.

"I have told you. You are almost five, and your father will soon take charge of your care."

"But I don't want to go with him. I want to stay with you."

"You will grow to be a man under his instruction; it is our custom." Sartaña answered, trying to be positive but secretly dismayed by the lessons and morals Katari would seek to instill in their son. How would a spirit like Theron's fare under such a dark, self-serving mentor? Could she be bent, twisted, and altered to his will? As these questions passed through Sartaña's mind for the thousandth time, she had a vision of Inti—knife in hand, claiming his first head as a leader and warrior, with Katari standing over him, directing and demanding. It was a picture not of the future, but an image of what the father would wish to see, how he would school his son. It was at that moment that Sartaña knew she must take Katari's life.

"Will I still see you?" Inti wanted to know.

"I will never leave you," Sartaña said as she knelt before her son, looking into his eyes. "Follow your instincts, child. Always do what you know to be right, and the heavens will smile on you. You are special, Inti. You come from a long line of healers and priests. If you listen, your intuition, your spirit-voice, will never lead you astray. Stay open and loving and trust your inner wisdom . . . and you will be loved, a gift to our people."

Only five yards away, Katari contemplated the mother and son. He had come looking for them to have Inti join him on a survey of the outer boundaries, and now he stood listening, hidden by a narrow wall.

Katari's ire was raised. Sartaña had served her purpose. The time had come to eliminate her influence.

Katari walked away without revealing himself.

The Emissary is defeating you! the Beast growled, but Katari's Helghul-brain was calm and methodical. Soon he would enact the second stage of his scheme, and Inti would be his to mold. Together, he and Theron would be the most feared and prolific conquerors of all time.

Chapter 13

Dim Traces of Light

Without warning, Sartaña's door burst open, and Katari entered in swift strides, startling her. The guard, who had become familiar over the years, flashed a concerned glance at Sartaña as he closed the door. The sentinel had always been kind, and had benefited from Sartaña's compassion and expertise when his own children had fallen ill. He was a good-hearted man, a husband and a father, and he liked Inti and Sartaña, having witnessed what a loving mother she was.

Sensing the gravity of the unexpected incursion, Sartaña lowered herself from her seat and bowed her head, kneeling.

"I see that you seek to ingratiate yourself," Katari laughed, seething with contempt. He paced her quarters, his square frame puffed up, appearing twice his size, as if ready to do battle. The shrunken heads, her husband's included, jiggled sickeningly on his belt, like charms.

"Tell me, Marcus, what do you remember of Atitala?" Katari asked, ignoring the guard as if he were not there. Sartaña's Marcus-memory had grown clearer and stronger, but she had no intention of helping Helghul.

"I don't understand," she lied.

"We were once brothers. We can help each other. If you tell me the location of the Emerald Tablet, I will give you Inti," Katari bargained. "If you continue to feign ignorance, you will never see him again."

Sartaña didn't know where the Emerald Tablet was. Marcus had not seen it since leaving Atitala. She wished that she knew.

Would she give it to Helghul in exchange for her son— her soulmate?

"I would help you if I could, High Priest, but I do not have the information you seek," she said, desperately regretting ever saying his name and letting him know that she had memory. It had been a terrible, naive mistake.

Sartaña looked up from where she knelt and was sent reeling as the leather of his foot smashed into her face. She was lifted off the floor, and her head slammed against the stone wall behind her. She cradled her skull in her hands. Her cheek was red and bruised where she'd been kicked. She hung her head, unable to stop her tears, and she dared not look at Katari again.

"You have served your purpose. Inti has bridged the gap between our people. I have reestablished Stone-at-Center as a profitable hub of trade, and I have gained even more through exploiting the weak-minded flock that seeks spiritual enlightenment and answers here. I couldn't have managed this without your help," he scoffed.

"But now you are done . . . a ghost . . . dead. As of tomorrow, the city will be informed of your untimely death . . . a budding pregnancy gone horribly wrong. With no woman to help you, you tried bravely to tend to yourself, and you bled to death in the process. They will grieve for you, saddened that you died giving birth to my stillborn child. They will pity me, and I will hang my head in mock grief. I have arranged for a wrapped body to be mourned in your absence—"

"My absence?" she interrupted. "You will not kill me?"

"Kill you? No, I like to know exactly where my enemies are, Marcus. If I release your soul back into the grid, there is no controlling when you'll show up again . . . I don't want any surprises from you. I like the idea of keeping you, like a head on my belt, under my control."

"Inti—" she began.

"My son is no concern of yours. To him, as to everyone else, you are dead."

"It doesn't have to be like this," Sartaña pleaded.

"No, it doesn't, and perhaps if you were more helpful, sharing information about the Emerald Tablet, things would be different. Until then, this is how I want it." He approached Sartaña menacingly, and she reacted like a cornered animal, no longer subservient or compliant. The fury in every cell of her body radiated hatred, and her Marcus-brain regretted that she had not tried to eliminate Katari before now. She could have poisoned his wine, or put a knife to his throat as he slept. She might have died trying, but instead she had allowed Katari to unravel his evil plan. She had handed him control of her precious Inti: her dear Theron.

Sartaña shuddered as she considered what Helghul would do to the spirit of her child. What kind of minion would he seek to create, and would he destroy the boy in the process? She frantically looked around for a weapon. She would end him if she could.

There was no weapon except for those attached to Katari. Sartaña lunged at his legs, attempting to bowl him over. The diminutive woman was no match for the steady man, and reflexively, the warrior defended with a powerful kick to her jaw. Sartaña rebounded with a thud, cracking her skull as she landed. Everything went black.

Katari knelt in front of her, concerned that he may have killed her in his rage. He found that she was still breathing, so he unsheathed the cradle-shaped copper blade from his side, swiftly bringing it to her face. Her small room was gory with blood by the time Katari finished his evil work, and he wrapped her in bloody sheets and carried her out past the worried guard.

"It is important that no one here ever suspect that she remains alive. Inti must never know. You and I alone know the truth. You will guard the High Priestess the rest of her days. The lives of your wife and children depend on your secrecy," Katari said.

Katari acted like a distressed husband and father as he moved through the palace toward the sacred subterranean temple where all religious ceremonies and rites were performed. Stone heads adorned the walls of the sanctuary, reflecting the variety of faces from around the Earth.

Sartaña awoke alone, unable to move, in severe pain, on the floor of a prison cell. Her head felt like a swollen, pulpy mess, and she couldn't move or work her jaws at all. She had vague recollections of someone pouring water into her mouth and forcing her to drink, even though it was excruciating. Her world was agony, and only the total disconnection of unconsciousness gave her any reprieve.

On the third day, she woke for a longer period of time and was able to sit. Her head felt like she wore a crown of thorns, and she wobbled dizzily. Her body ached and burned for food. She was grateful when the guard opened the door to deliver water to her. She recognized him from her former chamber. He was kind, and she could tell by his eyes that he was distressed by what he saw.

Sartaña tried to speak but was unable. She had been horribly disfigured—there were deep lacerations healing on her face. She had a broken jaw as well. Her guard had bandaged her head and chin. She had the strange sensation that her mouth was oddly hollow and cotton-filled at the same time.

She could only moan and make sounds from her throat, and she tried to use her tongue to assess the damage. She couldn't find it. Her mind reeled in confusion. *She couldn't find her tongue!* She willed it to move, and nothing: her mouth was empty and still. She couldn't feel her teeth or the roof of her mouth; there was no sensation at all. She frantically raised her hands, pushing against the bandages despite the blinding bolts of pain that reverberated through her head.

"Stop, Priestess! Leave it!" the distressed guard begged, but Sartaña anxiously opened her slack, splintered jaw. Nothing: only a sickening stump where her tongue should have been. Katari had said he would silence her.

Sartaña moaned from her throat as the guard gently rebandaged her. How had she allowed this? How had she been so naive as to believe that Katari would show her mercy? Her mind was filled with murder. There had been so many opportunities when she could have killed Katari, but she'd been unwilling to take on the karmic weight of committing murder or risk losing a single moment with Inti. She wondered now if killing Katari would have been for the greater good. Had it been Marcus's purpose as an Emissary to protect these people and their world from Katari's foul influence? Had he failed? Sartaña regretted not killing the tyrant, and it would haunt her for many years to come that Katari walked freely, terrorizing her son and her people while she lay useless in a cell.

The jail was near the center of the city. When Sartaña was well enough to stand, she could almost touch all of the sandy rock walls of her cell at one time. She was grateful for a tiny square opening high on one wall and, though it did not allow her to look out, late in the afternoon it let in a single beam of daylight. The sunbeam was high above her, but if she stood on her toes, her fully outstretched fingertips could just enter the opening, feel the sun's warmth, and churn its shining particles as they rained down.

The tiny jail was almost empty. Katari did not believe in feeding and maintaining those who broke his laws or who opposed his views. His retribution was typically swift and final. Sartaña was confined alone. She was isolated and tended by just one guard.

Sartaña existed on a diet of water and a mealy broth with dry bread, and she languished, miserably tormented by the predicament of her child. Only the kindness of her guard sustained her. It was he who filled her mouth with pain-relieving minced leaves and dressed her injured jaw. His kindness was extended through simple communication. He provided the contact that she craved, and he kindly offered her updates about Inti, even though doing so put him in jeopardy.

Inti believed her to be dead. *Oh, the pain he must be feeling—the anger, the mourning—and with only Katari to console him!* Sartaña's Marcus-brain was tormented to once again be parted from Theron. The pain was made worse by the injustice of mother and child being purposely separated. It didn't matter what she thought; Katari was the father, the High Priest. He had the power to do as he wished, and Sartaña knew that he had planned it all along. He had fooled her with indifference, convinced her to raise the boy and help win over the city. She had been duped into teaching Inti their ways, and Katari had planned to eliminate her all along. Her throat burned hoarse, dry, and thick with anguish, and she placed her desperate forehead on the filthy stone floor and begged for relief.

Sartaña's Marcus-consciousness understood that there was great learning in suffering, but she struggled to see her lesson. *What could this hell be teaching her? Loss? Seething hatred? Was this deep suffering a consequence of the Bronze Age slipping into the Iron?* She wished Marcus was a warrior on the battlefield fighting Helghul. She wondered if Katari had the advantage because of the Age they were in. *Would Helghul have the upper hand over the Emissaries in this Dark Age, no matter what?*

Sartaña battled with her misery, but when she was calm enough to meditate, her mind escaped to her higher self. It was there that she found stillness, tranquility, and the strength to power on. The priestess took solace in what remained of her limited voice. She had been reduced to the original primordial words of the universe. From her gut, "Ah"; from her throat, "Uh"; and from her lips and nose, "Mmm." The vibration of *Aum* or *Om* also brought her some peace. It reminded her of the true nature of reality and helped her to feel connected in her isolation.

Sartaña realized that, given the choice, she would not change her predicament if it meant not finding Theron, or not feeling the mother love she felt for Amaru and Inti. This realization led to a new kind of acceptance, and in the blackest moments of her despair, there was a light, as the love in her heart encouraged her to go on. Marcus was learning something, after all.

As the days wore on, Sartaña regained her strength, determined to escape. She planned to somehow retrieve her son and get away from Katari so they could become the Emissaries they were meant to be.

><< ><< ><<

Inti had been inconsolable when Katari had informed him of Sartaña's death. The child had not yet realized that he and his mother were separate people. He could not comprehend that she had gone somewhere he could not go, and above all, he could not understand why she had left without saying goodbye. The child had begged to see her and was permitted to view the wrapped corpse laid out for the vast multitudes of mourners who came from a great distance to pay their respects. Inti insisted that his mother was not in the wrappings, and did not understand that being dead meant that his mother was gone forever. He became angry and demanded that the gods bring her home. He promised to be a good son, sure that he had somehow done something to cause it all. Katari played on his son's grief and uncertainty, strategically giving and withdrawing his attention to manipulate the boy.

Sartaña's funeral pyre had been the highest in the history of Stone-at-Center, and after her cremation, the citizens had mourned for the prescribed twenty days. Katari had been thrilled with the economic benefits—the gifts the wailing pilgrims had offered. He had ensured that the mourning did not interfere with commerce.

With Sartaña gone, Inti was despondent and sullen, and Katari quickly lost patience with him, expecting him to behave as a much older child might. The Beast within Katari criticized the bond that had been allowed to grow between Inti and Sartaña. His Helghul-brain was once again twisted by jealousy; allowing Marcus and Theron any contact with each other had been a mistake, regardless of how well it had worked in his favor as ruler. He vowed never to make the same mistake again.

Inti spent every day at his father's side and was determined to please him. He quickly learned to hide his grief and compassion. The young boy soon began to walk like Katari, in the same wide, bowlegged swagger, with a thick stick whacking the ground. Like his father, he took what he wanted from merchant carts without permission or payment. He swatted at people or animals that impeded his path or even came too near. Katari was creating a miniature of himself, and the more satisfied he became, the more Inti's behavior was molded.

But while the rest of her kingdom believed her to be dead, Sartaña was healing. The trauma of losing a second son to Katari consumed her thoughts. Her Marcus-brain reminded her that she still had a purpose and needed to think about escaping. She was alive; therefore, her journey was not finished. Updates about her son's well-being, relayed to her by her kindhearted guard, slowly rekindled her faith in humankind.

✁ ✁ ✁

Years passed, and Inti's recollections of his mother faded, though he tried desperately to catalog and preserve each one of them. There were no sculptures or drawings—nothing in her likeness—and his father refused to speak of her at all. The son no longer remembered the curve of his mother's jaw, the shape of her eyes, or the feel of her hand in his. Despite the lost memories, he remained tied to her, constantly hearing her words in his head as if she was in the room with him: *Follow your instincts,* he heard. *You are special. You will be a great, compassionate leader. A gift to our people.*

Initially, after Sartaña was mourned, the people had looked to Katari, hopeful that he and Inti would fill the spiritual void Sartaña had left behind. Katari, however, was unable and unwilling to put the needs of the people before his own. The citizens endured oppression and poverty while Katari's personal fortune grew. Trade once again slowed as surrounding areas grew protective and wary of the threat Katari posed.

People who dared to speak out were killed. Small groups of insurgents who raided Katari's crops for food were captured and hunted for sport in macabre competitions and games. Many of Katari's own Puma-warriors became disgruntled. Now citizens and fathers themselves, they struggled to feed their families and were too often run ragged during brutal campaigns, with little personal reward. Like the other citizens, they watched Katari's comfort grow while they toiled and starved. Katari felt nothing for them. There was no trauma horrible enough to move him. The empathy that Helghul had surrendered allowed him to embrace his most dark and selfish tendencies, and the Beast provided many such inclinations.

Inti was only aware of his current life. His Theron-brain was completely forgotten, and though his purpose as an Emissary flowed within him, it only represented whispers, compared to the daily shouting of Katari. Inti wanted to become the leader that his father promised he could be. But still, Sartaña reached out to him telepathically, helping to stoke his inner Theron-nature, and subconsciously, Inti heard her.

Katari was determined to use Inti as a tool of his own will. When Inti questioned him in the face of simple commands, which no one else would have dared to do, the leader was deliberately patient, determined to undermine and reprogram his son's natural tendencies.

Without Sartaña present to temper Katari's influence, Inti was taught to reject his innate character. The contrasting influences of the light within the Emissary, versus Katari's constant brainwashing, engulfed the boy in confusion. Inti struggled to manage the duality of his life. When compassion or empathy did seep through, Inti would respond by lashing out harshly, embracing his shadow side to please his father.

"Remember, you must always survey the danger," Katari instructed while they were on a hunting expedition in his son's tenth year. Inti was already an expert with his sling and could down a screaming monkey at twenty paces. He had learned to skin and cook the animal, which tasted good but looked alarmingly like a human on the roast.

"In peace and in war, it is always better to let your underlings go before you," his father said as they walked.

"That seems like a cowardly act. I would lead!" Inti said, to impress his father, still carefully scanning the horizon for prey.

"Bravery is for the simpleminded. It is the meal we feed our warriors to reinforce them and make them do what we want. A leader must be smart. Never risk yourself when there are others to incur that risk. That is the power of being the king. That is how the clever lead, how they survive to maintain a kingdom. *Our* lives are *more* important," Katari said.

Inti had often seen this philosophy in practice. Katari would sacrifice the lives of his warriors without a second thought. He trusted no one; and suspected everyone of selfishness, treason, and dishonor. Inti wondered if Katari would protect him. Would he die for his son?

Do what you must! Dispose of this Emissary, and be done with it! the Beast had ordered. Katari understood the power of these inner voices and urgings and constantly anticipated and countered the inner voices he knew also besieged Inti. He watched the Emissary carefully, always gauging how best to manipulate and control him. In lifetimes to come, Helghul would use every shred of knowledge he had gained.

"That voice you hear in your head, telling you to be merciful and sacrificial, is an evil demon sent to fool you! It will be your undoing as king. It will doom your people if you are weak and cannot do what you need to do despite the unpleasantness of the task. It is like the first time you had to skin a monkey. You cried like a baby," Katari said.

Inti's eyes flashed in embarrassment at the remembrance, and he scowled at his father.

"But now you are proficient at it! You will skin many monkeys in life. A ruler must endure much in order to do what needs to be done."

Inti glowed at the compliment.

Katari had continued to expand his lands, and he planned to take his son along on the next campaign to begin his lessons as a warrior. There was much to be done before Inti would be ready for the ruthlessness of combat. He would eliminate anything and anyone his son cared for. Would he become bitter? Was an Emissary subject to the same responses as other people? Could he break an Emissary's will?

Katari had already taken Sartaña away, and he had made sure there were no servants or guards who held any special meaning for the boy. Katari alone was his mentor, confidant, and friend. No one else could get close. Inti was isolated and came to believe that his father was the only person in the world he could rely on.

When Inti was ten, Katari was informed of an interaction that caused him to increase the intensity of Inti's instruction. Inti had been walking through the marketplace of Stone-at-Center surrounded by three Puma-warriors, his head high, and feeling superior to those around him.

The boy overheard a pottery merchant with a llama cart full of product bartering with an herb merchant whose wares were laid out across his back-sling on the ground.

"My daughter is very ill, and these herbs can heal her. If I pay what you ask, my young child will go hungry," the pottery merchant explained.

"I have children, also. I have carried these herbs from the jungle. I need food, not clay pots," the herb seller said. He was not unmoved by his neighbor's plight; he was simply more concerned with his own.

At the sight of the young prince and his intimidating companions, the merchants became silent, waiting for them to pass by. Few people outside the palace had the courage to address Inti, and the boy was pleased by the power he wielded.

"Listen here," Inti said.

"Your Highness," the pottery merchant replied while the humble herbalist remained silent, believing that his low position, ragged clothes, and filthy hands made him beneath the boy's notice.

"Is that your llama?" Inti asked the merchant, gesturing with his stick.

The man's eyes popped open with concern. *What if the prince takes my llama? What, then?*

"Yes, Prince," the merchant replied, looking from the stern warriors to their weapons.

"You, lend the healer your cart for two days, and he will be able to visit the river basin and return with the medicine more quickly and with a larger load. This exchange will benefit you both."

"You are wise," the pottery merchant told Inti.

"Many thanks, Prince," the herbalist said.

Inti felt that he was in command, pleased that he could help with the negotiation.

"You can each pay for my assistance with half of today's earnings. Return at sunset and collect from them," Inti said to the Puma-warriors. He felt a powerful surge, knowing that he had brokered the deal. It mattered not that an ill child would have her medicine. The merchants wished he hadn't intervened. They would both be at further loss, given the payment now due to Katari's coffers.

When the Puma-warriors relayed the interaction to Katari at the end of the day, they thought he would be impressed by Inti, but the leader was angry that Inti had cared to stop to save the child. He believed that Inti was masking the higher intentions of his inner self. The boy was proving to be more of a challenge to reshape than Katari had anticipated. *Theron's inner nature must not prevail!* In response to Inti's actions, Katari presented him with a fabulous and unusual gift.

"What is it?" Inti asked as he rushed to the covered basket at his father's side. Throwing the top aside, he uncovered a tiny black jaguar cub. The creature meowed and growled with hunger. Its sandpaper tongue licked, and its razor-sharp teeth searched for food.

"I named him Patha. It means 'the lesson.' Your ability to take care of this creature is practice for your time as king, when you will take care of an entire empire."

The boy fell instantly in love with his pet and held it in his lap, nursing it with alpaca milk fed through a leather skin. It was his. It loved him unconditionally, reminding him of another time, when he'd been loved like that. It was a mother he could barely remember. She had held him in her arms, just as he held his new pet. Inti was determined that he would do better. He would never fail Patha.

Katari was pacing, and Sartaña's words burned within him. *"You're a pawn, used by darker souls!"* Sartaña had shouted. *"Unloved,"* she'd said. Did she know how those words ate away at him? Was he a pawn to the Beast? Was he destined to be unloved? Helghul wondered if Marcus had truly been aware of the thoughts that tortured Helghul every day in every incarnation . . . or had it been a lucky guess?

The Emissary cannot be converted. You are wasting our time! Imprison the boy with the other Emissaries, the Beast demanded.

More and more as the Ages descended, the Beast bound to Helghul's soul interrupted his planning and mental processes with ideas of its own. Often Katari seamlessly integrated the Beast's suggestions and strategies, but other times he resisted, as his ego was injured, and struggling to assert his power within.

It is not for you to direct me, Helghul told the Beast. *The boy is young and still adapting to the environment. I can convert him, for as the Great Year cycle descends, even the Emissaries become more dense and fearful. I can feel their power diminishing.*

Do not underestimate them. When they join together, they are mighty, even in this time. The Jaguar sparks love within the Emissary, the Beast warned.

"The jaguar will never reach maturity," Katari said aloud, and these heartless words silenced the inner dialogue, however briefly.

Chapter 14

A Cruel Lesson

Patha slept in a basket near Inti nightly for the next four weeks. The boy took his new pet with him everywhere, and in private, he cuddled it with joy. It was a blissful pleasure he had long been denied. Not since Sartaña's reported death had Inti enjoyed the closeness and affection of another living creature. The most he ever received from Katari was an approving hand on his shoulder. Theron's soul blossomed lovingly within Inti, a side effect that Katari had anticipated and planned to exploit. The name Patha, the Sanskrit word for "lesson," had not been chosen lightly.

Inti seemed oblivious to the animal's natural threat, though more than once he nursed a scratch or incidental bite. The cat was still small, playful, and manageable, and Inti loved it wholeheartedly.

Katari had known the pet was impractical. He was aware that a full-grown jaguar would be impossible to manage. He had also known that it would never come to be.

"I cannot find Patha! I cannot find Patha!" Inti shouted down the corridors one morning. His heart raced when, after looking under every pile and object, his dear pet had not been found. He wondered if it had jumped out the high window into the court-yard below. Patha could be injured!

"Master?" a servant girl said, bowing as she approached. Inti pushed her roughly out of the way.

"My jaguar, he's gone! Call everyone to help find him," Inti demanded. The animal was far too young to be a threat. Soon, the entire staff of the grounds was calling and searching.

Katari had been up for hours. Early in the morning, he had quietly entered his sleeping son's room and removed the cat from beside the boy. He listened while the commotion in the hallways grew, and then there was a knock at his door.

"Come."

"Father, it's Patha. He's gone!" Inti lamented. He hadn't cried in many years—his father had not allowed it—but tears now flowed freely down his cheeks as he scanned the room hopefully.

"Not much of a king if you lose your kingdom," Katari said knowingly.

"I didn't lose him . . . I woke, and he was gone." The boy tried to hold back a sob to please his father.

"Tears will not bring him back. Do not let the people see you so weak and childlike. A jaguar has long been a symbol of power and strength. Collect yourself, and we will go find this animal together," Katari said patiently. Inti wiped his face and felt grateful for his father. He was going to help. He was the High Priest; he would make everything right again.

Together, they exited the palace, and one after another, the servants shook their heads, skittering from Katari nervously.

"No sign yet."

"He's not here."

"I will take my group to search the fields," a Puma-warrior answered sorrowfully, afraid to deliver bad news to the temperamental leader. No one wanted to bear the brunt of Katari's disappointment and suffer a beating, prison, or worse.

Inti and his father continued down the narrow stone stairway into the city. They were surrounded by the Puma-warriors, who were looking under bushes and peering through doorways. Inti continued to call out. Curious children scampered out of their way, and Inti commandeered them to help search. In awe of their young prince, they obeyed, aware that they had no other choice.

Four hours later they returned empty-handed, tired and sticky with dust and heat. They were approached by one of Katari's most trusted warriors. He whispered to the leader, who grimaced exaggeratedly in response.

"What is it? What did he say?" Inti asked, looking from his father to the glum messenger.

"They have found the thief; he's being held at the prison," Katari said.

"Prison? A thief? Someone took Patha?" It had not occurred to Inti that someone might have taken his animal. He had assumed the pet had simply escaped on its own.

"Prepare yourself. It's worse than we feared."

"Where is Patha?" Inti asked in confusion.

"He is dead, mutilated for his heart," Katari said, feigning sympathy, his Helghul-brain watching carefully for signs of the effect the news would have.

"I don't understand," the boy said blankly. He stumbled as they hurried toward the jail, and he was steadied by his father's quick hand.

"The prisoner tore the flesh from the helpless little creature in a sacrifice, to steal its strength for himself," Katari said brutally, needling his son.

"Are they sure? It might not be Patha. Patha is more likely hiding somewhere, exploring."

"When they found the criminal, he was covered in blood, and there were bits of the animal all around. They have the jaguar's head . . . you can see for yourself," Katari said.

Inti's stomach lurched at the prospect. "I'll know him. I'll know my Patha!"

From the beginning, his father had been clear. Patha had been the boy's responsibility, his kingdom to manage and take care of. Inti was overwhelmed by his guilt and his failure, though he continued to hope that Patha had been spared.

Inti ran the short and well-traveled path to the prison. Katari congratulated himself on his progress so far. The boy was responding just as he had intended. To what degree could Theron be bent to his will? What was an Emissary capable of if pushed?

The Puma-warriors followed closely behind Katari. Sartaña's guard bristled at the arrival of the High Priest, and pressed his back tight to the wall to get out of his way as he passed to the open chamber at the end of the longest corridor.

As always when Katari came, Sartaña could hear him from her cell and could see Helghul's shine flowing in dark currents around him. He would often walk the dim, putrid corridors and pound on her thick, wooden cell door, barking warnings and threats. There was a notch in the wood of her door that made it possible for her to watch, and often she did, but only to see her child.

Sartaña would hover near her door when she heard the High Priest enter, hopeful that Inti was close by. When her son was near, Sartaña reached for Theron's buoyant energy. Katari had ensured that Sartaña's cell was at the end of the hall, and he had made certain she could clearly hear the screams that echoed from the torture he delivered before new prisoners were taken to the central courtyard and publicly executed.

Inti had been present many times as his father had tortured prisoners. The first time was just after Sartaña's faked death, and he had closed his eyes and covered his ears to avoid hearing the cries of the victims. The scene had sickened the child, but Katari had insisted he stay. Helghul felt the Beast pushing him to be done with Theron, but the father was determined to harden his son; Helghul was determined to turn the Emissary to his will.

More than once since that first time, a weapon had been handed to the young boy. Inti had been forced to strike a prisoner while the king reminded him that as a leader, it was his duty to protect his people from criminals. It was his duty to "skin the monkey." Inti did not understand that he was as much a victim of his father as the captives were.

Sartaña was startled as she heard the commotion around Katari's entrance. He had been there earlier that morning, and it was unusual for him to come twice in one day. She peeked through the small sliver in her door and saw her son and the beautiful halo of color that surrounded him.

The air vibrated with Katari's dark, flowing shine. The High Priest pounded especially hard on Sartaña's door, desiring that she witness the scene that was about to be played out. She pressed her eye to the knot, watching Inti. His energy was strangely tumultuous, and his small hands were balled into fists at his sides.

Sartaña's soul reached out to him, and her heart and body ached to touch him—so close but yet so far, kept apart by a wood door. She longed to see his face, to hold his hands in hers, to hear his voice. *Turn around,* she called out wordlessly. *Look at me,* she begged. But she was without a tongue and had no ability to shout.

Despite his rage and confusion Inti felt a shiver, a tug at his instincts, that told him he was being watched. He turned his anxious gaze to her door and saw the eye pressed to the gap in the wood. It was so white that it seemed to glow, and he paused, inexplicably drawn to the eye that seemed to smile at him and that had strangely called to him.

The lump in Inti's throat bobbed and choked him. Katari felt his son losing his fury. He saw Sartaña's eye pressed to the door and became aware of their multicolored karmic shine mingling in the corridor. He felt the weak telepathic strand forming between them and irritably corralled his son forward, whispering dark words in his ear and glaring threateningly at the space where the eye had been moments before.

Katari barked orders as a prisoner was led into the chamber. The captive was heavyset, with dark, sun-worn skin, and his hair was alive with lice. His tunic and pants were covered in blood, and the stench of him forced his captors to suck in their breath in disgust. Katari ignored the bands of purple-and-indigo light that flowed beautifully in and around the man, mingling with the similar karmic colors that flowed around Inti—it was the shine of an Emissary, which only Helghul and Marcus could see.

Sartaña gasped as her Marcus-brain recognized one of her own, and she watched in horror, dreading what would come. The prisoner had once been an Atitalan. He was a familiar, beloved soul who stood out for Marcus among the students from long ago. *Bapoo!* Sartaña suddenly remembered his name, and though he wore a different suit of skin, he was still Bapoo to Marcus. But at present, he was nothing more than a tool in Helghul's experiment, a test of his ability to turn an Emissary. Marcus was filled with memories and wept for his old friend, while he sent him strength to endure what would certainly come.

"This man was found covered in blood and surrounded by the carcass of the jaguar cub. He's from a distant land. He speaks no language that we know," the captain of the Puma-warriors explained.

Though he feigned outrage, Katari had invented the story himself. The foreigner had been an ideal pawn. A stranger to Inti and therefore unable to plead, explain, or beg for mercy, he had come to Stone-at-Center as a pilgrim months earlier. Katari's Helghul-brain had identified the reincarnated Emissary, Bapoo, immediately, and he had detained him without explanation. The prisoner had languished, starving, in the prison, until Helghul finally found an evil use for him.

The prisoner, Bapoo, was thrown the dead carcass of Patha. In desperation, he had fallen upon the carrion for survival. Katari had watched merrily, his plan fully in motion.

Katari shoved the prisoner to his knees. Inti was shaking at his father's side, staring at the blood on the front of the captive's filthy clothing and chin.

"Where's my jaguar?" Inti demanded, clenching his jaw. The Emissary stared at him without understanding. Sartaña and Katari both wondered if Inti sensed Bapoo's energy. *Would Theron recognize one of her own?* The captive dared to glimpse at the child, and there was a flicker of compassion.

This boy is confused and forced, the Emissary thought with empathy, and Inti faltered.

"He murdered your Patha. Bring the head, the paws, the skin! He ate his heart like it was a tamarillo!" Katari said angrily, pacing around the Emissary on the floor. Inti couldn't help but imagine the juices of the red plumlike fruit dripping from the man's mouth.

Sartaña knew what Katari was doing. As always, he was twisting Inti and manipulating him. Katari handed his son a heavy, flat stone that barely fit in the boy's hand and nudged him forward, close enough to touch the prisoner. Inti trembled with rage, and his legs felt as though they might buckle.

The boy gulped as the Puma-warrior returned with the ghoulish head of the jaguar extended in his palm, too near his face. There could be no mistaking it. All sympathy left Inti; there was only anger remaining. He had been exposed to violence his entire life. It was a part of life and of survival, and in that moment, he was filled with murderous rage.

"Ripped apart while you slept . . . while you did not protect . . . ," Katari goaded, determined to inflame him further. The young prince swung the rock and hit the prisoner with a sickening thud. A large gash opened up in the man's head directly above his left eye as he fell to the dust.

Katari glowed with satisfaction. It was as he thought! Even Theron, daughter of White Elder, could be used and turned under the correct circumstances. What great power this knowledge gave him!

The injured Emissary looked up from the dirt, and Inti was overcome with sympathy upon seeing the fear and confusion in his eyes. The stranger seemed familiar, as his shine billowed and swirled, merging with his own. Inti turned his face away from the victim, and Sartaña silently called to him, calling for him to stop, praying that Inti's Theron-soul would not succumb to Helghul's manipulation.

Have mercy. You are good and kind . . . an Emissary. It is Bapoo, one of our own.

Inti stood shaking, rock in hand, unwilling to strike a second blow and unable to rouse himself to the anger and brutality required to continue. He was filled with grief for Patha, his heart so full of love for the creature that it ached within him. And that grief had turned to compassion for the man he had just struck. Katari, sensing that Inti had lost his rage, pushed him forward. Inti snapped his shoulder back and glared angrily at his father.

"That anger you feel is for *him*, not for me! He attacked your kingdom! Will Patha's murder go unavenged?" Katari shouted, but Inti remained frozen, trapped between two opposing worlds of thought. His empathy was stronger than his rage.

Angered by his son's mounting compassion, Katari snatched the rock from the boy in disgust and pushed him aside. Inti turned his head away as his father slammed the stone against the captive's yielding skull and sprayed them all with blood and grey chunks of brain. Though Inti's eyes were closed, the sound of the stone as it connected reverberated sickeningly through him.

The colorful bands emanating from the murdered Emissary hovered above him, collecting together. Bapoo, skinny and small, was visible in the bright specks of his shine as he stared down at his former body. He then slipped away like smoke, and his spirit was released to the place in between. Bapoo was once again a current, returning to the meadow and the grid until his next incarnation.

Sartaña was overcome by the cruelty and waste she had witnessed. She mourned the loss of such a good spirit in the world, though she knew the Emissary's absence was temporary.

Inti would not look at the battered skull, as a dark pool of blood spread slowly, covering the dirt and pebbles as it crept across the floor. Instead, he stared at Sartaña's door. The eye was there. Even from a distance, Inti could sense it watching them. He wondered briefly to whom the eye belonged.

Despite her grief for her bludgeoned ally, Sartaña knew that her son could see her, and she smiled. So rare was the occasion for her to smile that her scars pulled and stretched in complaint. Her lined skin creaked in protest, but she continued, seeing that Inti's eyes were kind, as they had always been. Sartaña was flush with pride that Inti had been unwilling to do as Katari had demanded.

Inti could not see the shine that had grown and flowed to join with his, but Sartaña felt her son's spirit reaching out to her. Theron's energy once again coupled with Marcus's, like a key in a padlock. Both child's and mother's skin erupted in gooseflesh.

Katari regrouped as the brightness of the auras doubled in the dim hallway. He saw Marcus's familiar shine swirling around Inti, and angrily he hurled the blood-covered stone against Sartaña's door. The High Priestess jumped back as it impacted with a thud, leaving a bloody imprint on the wood.

The tendrils of Sartaña's shine that had reached out, now retreated. She had seen and felt the colors of Inti and Bapoo, felt the familiar warmth and goodness that radiated from them. It was stronger than human touch, so deep, not just barely-there tingles but complete and overwhelming connections, and it was more than she had felt in many years. She had been alone for so long, reconciling her Marcus-memories and cataloging her previous lessons and lives. She had only seen her son from a distance through the sliver in her door, but this time they had connected.

Katari directed Inti toward the exit, leaving the warriors to clean up the carnage. Sartaña listened as her son was reprimanded by his father for being weak. She meditated, and inexplicably felt a new strength, reminded that she was not alone.

Chapter 15

A New Purpose

Sartaña was grateful when she finally heard the rustle of her cell door. She was hungrier than she had felt in years. Her guard stumbled as he entered and, grunting, kicked the ground at his feet. He placed a wooden bowl of water, quinoa, and a small chunk of dried llama meat on the floor. Other than a thin reed mat for sleeping, the cell was empty. Opposite the door, under the tiny window, ran a narrow, fetid ditch the length of the entire building. The putrid trough was occasionally flushed with dirty water to wash away the human waste that had collected there, but the stench never waned.

Sartaña's guard retreated, and once again stumbling, he kicked aside the stone that was tripping him up. The door closed with a clunk. Sartaña crouched to eat and felt the stone beside her. In the dark, she picked it up and felt the sticky blood and hair that clung to it. She remembered the crash of the rock against her door as Katari had thrown it hours before.

Sartaña dipped the corner of her tatty robe into her shallow water bowl, using almost all of her daily ration to soak the cloth. Respectfully, though she could not see in the darkness, the High Priestess washed away the gore, all the while praying for the Emissary whose blood had been so cruelly shed. The rock was round and smooth, and once clean, Sartaña decided that it must become an object of reverence to remember the brave life it had taken.

The High Priestess held the stone and meditated. Her interaction with Inti earlier in the day had lit a spark of hope within her. Sartaña's Marcus-brain was racing, and she prayed specifically for knowledge, to know what she should do. What *could* she do?

When Sartaña opened her eyes, a narrow ray of light from her high window was spanning the length of her tiny cell and cascading beautiful silver light particles in its path. The beam illuminated the shimmering, hoary dust in smooth, straight rows that appeared to rain down and disappear where the light left off. Sartaña was grateful for the beauty. It reminded her that she was still a part of a miraculous world. As she watched, the beam in one small section began to swirl and change, and she was mesmerized as she realized that a shape had formed. It was the familiar curve and arc of the Seed of Life. The dust moved and mingled until a small grid was invoked, and then it was gone. The sunbeam returned to its gravitational pull, returned to the silver rain, and Sartaña was left with the beautiful image in her mind.

Sartaña's Marcus-brain was at full attention and compelled her to take up the rock that she had so reverently scrubbed the night before. Sartaña looked at the rock in the light for the first time and knew what she would do. She would carve into the stone. She had a clear picture in her mind of the design. She would draw a group of seven identical circles that would form a flower with six petals. It was the same pattern that graced her shoulder and that freed her soul.

Sartaña's role as an Emissary began anew with this random, seemingly insignificant undertaking. She searched at the edge of her cell in the dirt and pebbles and tried each small shard as a tool until she found one sharp and dense enough to make a scrape in the smooth river rock. She worked devotedly for hours, then days, and she was amazed by the divine design that flowed so easily from her untrained hands. Sartaña had never been an artist or craftswoman, yet she had produced an extraordinary, geometrically perfect carving in only a week, with an inadequate tool and no ability to measure. It was truly miraculous.

The morning of the seventh day, Sartaña's guard entered to deliver her rations. The prisoner considered hiding the stone in her hand, but instead she hesitantly reached out, her palm open, and gave it to the guard, who turned it over and stared at her, dumbfounded.

"You carved this?" he asked, tracing the grooves in awe. She nodded tentatively. "Where is your blade?" he asked. Sartaña raised up the small, worn-out scrap of stone to him, and he shook his head in disbelief.

"High Priestess, you did this without a proper tool? It's not possible! It's perfect!" he proclaimed. Sartaña glowed at his response to her work. Without another word, the guard left, taking the stone with him. The woman feebly reached out to stop him, but the door closed with a clunk.

Sartaña was crestfallen; she had felt like her old self during the past week. She had experienced a sense of purpose and distraction that had eluded her during her imprisonment. She lay down on her mat and wondered if the kind guard would take her handiwork to Katari. It had been worth the risk. Considering how compelled she had been to create the carving, she knew that whatever happened was meant to be.

Sartaña was not alone for long. There was a rustle at her door, and she snapped upright in alarm. She was relieved as her guard entered with a secretive smile on his face. In his hands he held a bulky goatskin sack. He dropped the bag with a weighty clunk and unloaded a small pile of river rocks in the corner of the cell. Sartaña stared at him in astonishment as he handed her a sharp, crescent-shaped obsidian blade with a worn wooden handle.

"This was my father's . . . he was a skilled artisan and carved his whole life. This is a strong tool and should make your work much easier," he said proudly. Sartaña held the object like it was a precious gem, turning it over in her hands in disbelief.

"Don't hurt yourself," he added, glancing back and meeting her grateful eyes. She wished she could thank him. Sartaña knew that if Katari discovered what the guard had done, he would kill him. Her guard was a good, brave man.

Sartaña made her way to the heap of stones and chose one. She raised it to the heavens in blessing, and her mind flashed with visions from her many past lives. When finally she settled on one image, she began to scrape, scrape, scrape. She was a whirlwind, overcome with purpose and expertly carving with a skill she had never learned.

Day after day, week after week, month after month, Sartaña churned out the spectacular etchings at an impossible pace. She engraved images from Marcus's past lifetimes, concepts that no one of her time or land had ever dreamed of.

There were days when Sartaña almost ceased to exist, fully transmuted to the higher part of herself. She carved stories, ideas, experiments, celestial maps, centuries of knowledge—deep into the indigenous river rock. Her guard had begun leaving her cell door ajar, and the light and warmth from his fire comforted her and danced in patterns on the walls. He would sit next to the opening with his back pressed to the outer wall while she carved, and he'd tell her stories about Inti.

As the days passed, he shared humorous and interesting stories about his own children and family, as well as the daily events in the city. Sartaña loved the sound of his voice and worked in a new state of contentment. More than once, he shared a hallucinogenic drink with her, which helped her visions and creativity to bloom.

The guard continued to bring fresh stones and take the completed art away. Sartaña didn't care what happened to them; they would end up where they needed to be. Her job was to produce them, as prodigiously and prolifically as possible. What she did not know was that she was manufacturing her own possibility for escape, and she was not alone in her task. Other people nearby, Emissaries like her, were also busily carving without training or cause, but with a burning determination and in complete awe of the results of their toil. They, too, were being guided by their unconscious higher selves, though they did not know it at all. The Emissaries were often confused and disturbed by the foreign images they were producing, but they were compelled to continue.

The stones began to turn up in Stone-at-Center. Citizens found them and marveled at their intricacy and bizarre images. The community embraced them as signs from the gods that were riddled with messages too grand for them to understand, and they took them to their High Priest to decode. Initially, Katari dismissed the stones, intrigued but unconcerned by the images, assuming they were remnants from a time long past, a Golden Age he had known well and did not fear.

Katari's interest in the stones changed as they grew quickly in number, and the entire community could speak of nothing else. One afternoon, Katari was handed a specimen that caused him considerable alarm. The image was of a young warrior aiming a spear at the belly of an older man. In the sky above, there were three stars. The boy was wearing the headdress of a High Priest, and on his forehead was the eye of protection in the center of a triangle. Unlike the other stones that he had disregarded, Katari pulled this stone aside and kept it hidden in his chamber, disturbed by its imagery and its resemblance to both Inti and himself.

People continued to bring the perplexing stones to their leader, and his uneasiness grew. He was given another specimen that depicted a young boy in a High Priest headdress marked with the eye of protection, sitting on what was unmistakably a throne.

The next day, after a restless night plagued by nightmares, Katari decreed that all of the artisan stones were to be brought to him. As an incentive, he offered small sacks of grain. The High Priest also outlawed the production of the stones, declaring that anyone caught carving them would be put to death.

"Why do you care about a pile of rocks?" Inti asked, curious about his father's growing obsession.

"Have you heard them called the 'magic stones' or the 'sacred stones'?" Katari asked.

Inti could only nod, his mouth bursting with half-chewed meat.

"Doesn't that concern you? Have you learned nothing from me?" his father snapped irritably.

Inti retreated into silence while he ate, seething with anger and embarrassment at the reprimand. He was tougher than his Father believed. He would show him that he could be a mighty leader just like Katari. He continued to hear his mother's words: *Trust your instincts. You will be a great and well-loved leader, a gift to our people.*

He didn't care about being loved by the people. He cared more about pleasing Katari and becoming a powerful leader. He didn't miss Sartaña—he barely remembered her—but he did wonder what life might have been like if she hadn't died and left him. Would she be ashamed of the person he had become? Was he ashamed of himself?

Katari was despised by his subjects. Selfish and coldhearted, he had continued to claim the greatest part of his city's wealth and crops for himself. He ran the sacred sites and temples like a business. For thousands of years, Stone-at-Center had been open to all people. Katari had changed that, limiting access and requiring "donations" of cocoa beans, grains, peanuts, and cloth. No one could enter without paying his toll, and many were turned away— the sick, the elderly—even after days and weeks of travel. The High Priest had become powerful and rich, continually expanding his lands through commerce and force, but the people were left with barely enough to survive. Inti was increasingly aware of the discontent in the kingdom, but what could he do?

After they finished eating, father and son stretched their thick frames and belched, so similar in body but not in soul. Katari continued to lecture about the danger of allowing people to indulge in creative thinking. The images on the stones inspired deep contemplation.

"What people can imagine, they will seek to create. To keep them subservient, we must squash this creative force. We must keep them concentrated on fear and survival," Katari said. He knew that if people imagined a life beyond what he was willing to allow them, they would be restless and difficult to control.

Inti listened in silence, trying to learn, but his father's way of thinking seemed illogical to him. The boy didn't want to lose any of his comfort or power, but he wondered if the abundance could be shared more equally. He imagined a different way of living, but he knew that to raise these questions would also raise Katari's ire.

Father is cunning and wise. There must be a reason, Inti thought.

As the weeks went on, mounds of stones were collected and delivered to the palace. There were many of poor quality, carved without purpose or skill to gain a sack of grain, but it was the other stones, innovative and fantastic, that continued to confound Katari. It couldn't be Marcus; Sartaña remained securely neutralized, he had made certain of it. Helghul knew the scenes of flight, healing surgeries, and star alignments, and he recognized the ancient knowledge, but he could not understand the purpose of the stones. *Where they were coming from, and how were the artisans eluding his Puma-warriors?*

The number of stones grew and rubbed him like a blister; the leader arranged for them to be secretly carted far away from the city and placed deep in a cave.

Sartaña continued to work feverishly, inspired, unaware that mounds of stones came and went. Her guard continued to smuggle out her finished work and supply her with fresh stones, and he spent hours talking to her.

Like the other citizens, the guard believed that the stones were special. He told Sartaña about the rocks turning up en masse, and she was bewildered. Her confusion quickly turned to happiness at the realization that she wasn't alone. It was the confirmation that her path, though it seemed insignificant, must have a purpose greater than she could understand. There were others like her who were compelled to tell the stories in the stone. She was surprised to learn that Katari had proclaimed the rocks illegal, and she was worried for the safety of her guard. He never knew of her concern, but he put her at ease when he expressed his gratitude for the extra food and clothing that the stones provided his family.

It was a warm spring morning and the sun was punching through the small vent in Sartaña's cell when her guard made an announcement. "I am going to get you out of here, High Priestess. I've been looking for a way," the guard said.

Sartaña wished that she could speak, and her eyes implored him to continue.

"Thanks to your rocks, I have put aside a small reserve of supplies. I have procured a cart, and I will soon have enough to trade for a llama. I intend to take you and my family in the night and leave here."

Sartaña placed her hand over her mouth, and her eyes shone with gratitude, but she shook her head. She was grateful for the kindness of the man, but she knew she wouldn't leave. Not without Inti.

"Inti," the guard said, and Sartaña nodded. "I have considered it. I will try to convince him to come." Sartaña's eyes opened in alarm. "Don't worry, Priestess. I will be careful," he said, reading her concern.

The guard knew that it would be dangerous to approach Inti—possibly fatal—but he would do what was necessary. Sartaña didn't deserve her punishment, and now that he had the means, he was determined to get her and his family as far away from Katari as possible.

The guard plotted for weeks how he would approach Inti, and just when he thought getting the prince alone would be impossible, the problem was solved for him.

Inti had been walking with the High Priest and his entourage of warriors to survey the farmlands and the budding crops. The Beast within him had been especially irritated lately and demanded to be free of the overwhelming shine emanating from the Emissary.

If it were up to me, the boy would be long dead! You're a fool to keep this Emissary around, the Beast said.

Katari couldn't deny it. His Helghul-brain could see by Inti's shine that, despite his best efforts, Theron's energy was growing subtly stronger every day. Certainly Inti still talked and walked like him, kicking rocks, swinging the staff in his hand, and rudely barking orders, but Theron's light was increasing.

Katari's Helghul-brain was struggling to suppress the Beast's primal urgings. He might kill the boy—probably he would—but not yet. Inti was young, and he was no threat. Helghul knew Theron's spirit well, and she had no memory that would make her dangerous. Katari would wait, but he was prepared to execute the Emissary if necessary.

Do not make me suffer this putrid energy. It pours from him like light from the sun, the Beast said, and Katari agreed. He manufactured a reason for Inti to return to the palace. It was a relief to be free of the boy, and Katari plunged into his own darkness.

Inti quickly made his way back toward the city, excited to be free of his father's rhetoric. But in his haste and distraction, he tripped. He was unable to catch himself; the stick in his hand fell away, and he sprawled awkwardly onto the uneven path, twisting his right ankle. Katari hated when he was clumsy. Inti was relieved that his father had not been there to witness his bumbling.

His wrist, elbow, and knee were all bleeding and scraped, and he attempted to get up. Pain shot through his leg, and he turned over and sat, his eyes squeezed so that he wouldn't cry. *How would he walk now?* He held his injured ankle gently in his hands. It was then that he saw what had tripped him. He picked up a stone, shocked to see that it was intricately carved. It was one of the so-called sacred stones, just lying on the path.

It was unlike any of the others that he had seen before. It was simply the image of a flower, each of the six petals exactly the same size and surrounded by a perfect circle. There was not a gap, a chip, or a single spot that was not precisely balanced, and it sparked a faint memory.

Inti knew that he was going to have to walk, injured ankle or not. Using both hands, he carefully got to his feet and retrieved his walking stick while still holding the rock. He was pleased that the pain in his ankle had diminished slightly, but he knew he must not turn it again. With care, he began to limp back toward the city.

Up ahead, he was relieved to see a llama. He called out to the man beside it, who appeared to be rearranging a bulky pouch slung over the animal's back. The man came to help Inti but grew increasingly anxious as he approached and realized who had called him. The man nervously looked at the stone in Inti's hand, and the boy's eyes flashed to the pouch on the llama. Barely visible, beneath the flap, he saw another stone.

"Where did these come from? Who's making them?" Inti asked inquisitively, holding out the stone that was still in his hand. The guard looked at him pensively, and Inti understood.

"Don't be afraid," Inti said, placing a reassuring hand on the man's shoulder. "I want to know where the rocks come from. I don't want to harm you. This will be between us."

"It would be better if I *show* you, Prince."

Inti agreed, and once he was seated on the animal, the guard slung the heavy pouch of stones over himself and led the llama back to the village.

Inti was bursting with curiosity. The pair didn't speak while they hustled along the dusty trail to the jail. Inti wondered if he was being careless, possibly putting himself in danger, but he intuitively trusted the man. He understood that the guard was in far more danger than he was, should Katari discover them.

Inti was a prince, the heir to a significant empire with power and influence. Would he give it up for a mother he could barely remember and a guard who might be planning a ransom or worse? Those were serious considerations in these dark times, and he was still a child. Would Inti feel bound to his father?

The guard realized the enormity of what he was undertaking. He was about to irreversibly change his life and hopefully the lives of Sartaña and Inti as well. If the reunion of mother and son went well, they would plan their escape. If Inti refused, the consequences would be grave. Despite the danger to himself, the guard knew it was the right thing to do, and he led Inti to the prison.

"The artisan is in there?" Inti asked, surprised. He climbed off the llama and winced upon landing. Inti felt a strange energy rising in his belly. They entered, and Inti limped toward Sartaña's cell. When the guard finally stopped, the boy recognized the door where the eye had watched from months before, on the day of Patha's death.

Sartaña heard the familiar sound of her door being unlocked. The familiar face of her guard came around the edge of the door. He stepped aside, and Inti, squinting in the dim light to make out the figure, came eye to eye with Sartaña. She was awful—an ugly old crone. Her filthy black hair was streaked with grey, and the knobby, ridged scars that patterned her face made her distressing to look at. Her heart leapt and pounded in anticipation.

Sartaña stared in astonishment, filled with overwhelming love and joy. She did not move, and more than ever, she was tormented by the loss of her tongue. Her inability to speak at that moment was exactly the reason why the cruelty had been perpetrated. The guard backed himself out of the chamber, and Inti turned in alarm.

"I will return shortly, Prince," the guard said, raising his hand to assure the boy.

Inti was left alone with Sartaña. He looked around the cell and did his best to ignore the overpowering smells that were part of life there.

The guard hadn't told Inti anything. He had reasoned that it was better that Inti discover Sartaña for himself. If he recognized her, and pitied her, his emotions might make him more likely to join them and would leave less chance of alerting Katari.

"Did you do this?" Inti held out the stone with the seed of life toward her.

Sartaña nodded emphatically, smiling her broken, damaged smile. She recognized the first stone she had carved. It had brought them together!

The room was alive around them. Inti couldn't see the shine, but their auras danced and mingled, elated to be reunited. He felt it, this energy, and he went to her. He crouched in front of her.

"I have seen it before, but I don't know where. What does this symbol mean?" he asked, his young throat closing with emotion as their eyes locked, only inches apart.

She put her hand to her throat and shook her head, indicating her inability to speak. His pity for her compounded.

"Who are you?" he asked, searching her face, knowing she could not answer.

She took his young hand in hers. He allowed it and did not mind the dirty, cracked frailty of her grasp. Her mind screamed out to him. *My son! My Theron!* She projected all of her energy desperately into his. *He doesn't know me!* she thought in anguish. *Theron doesn't know me!* Sartaña's Marcus-brain acknowledged painfully. The deposed priestess maintained her composure and calm demeanor, afraid to scare him away.

Inti stared into her face, and he could tell she wanted to tell him something. The urgency in her eyes beseeched him. Suddenly she knew what to do, and she pushed up her ragged sleeve to expose the marking on her shoulder. Her son's recognition was immediate. He looked from the flower symbol branded on her skin to the rock, and back at her disfigured face.

"No!" he croaked, barely able to breathe. "It's you!" Inti's mind raced. "How is this possible? It can't be!" The colors around them were frenzied as his conscious emotions joined his unconscious ones.

Sartaña nodded emphatically, bringing his hand to her lips. Her tears poured down her ruined cheeks. Her face was luminous and filled with love.

Marcus and Theron had been reunited!

Inti embraced the frail ghost, and their souls danced and bubbled, sending pleasant shock waves through them. She felt like a skeleton in his arms, and his concern and sadness for her condition welled up in him.

"I thought you were dead. They told me you were dead!" he cried, tears flowing down his face.

Sartaña just shook her head and held him until his violent sobbing subsided.

"Why?" he asked angrily. "What happened? Why were you sent here?" Sartaña's joy turned to heartache as she once again imagined her young son mourning her.

"I want answers!" he shouted toward the door. The guard reentered, now unsure that he had done the right thing but knowing they must hurry. He was further alarmed by the vision of the young man before him, so distraught and wild-looking.

"You! Guard!" Inti yelled, grabbing the man with his free hand, the other hand still tightly clasping the flower-carved stone. "Tell me everything you know!"

The guard hesitated for a moment, then responded, "The High Priestess is of royal, sacred lineage. Your father claimed her and killed her husband and her son, your half brother, when he conquered this city. You were born one year later. When you were five, your father took over your care, and your mother was brought here."

"Who knows this? Who knows she lives?" Inti asked through gritted teeth.

"Only the three of us and the High Priest. He disfigured her and cut out her tongue so that she could never speak against him. I nursed her as best I could, but you see what a mess he made."

"It is your tongue I should have cut out," interjected Katari's deep menacing voice from behind the guard. In a flash, the point of Katari's spear burst through the startled man's chest. Inti let out a scream as the guard dropped to the floor with a heavy thud. He would not return to his family or make his escape. None of them would.

Sartaña and Inti recoiled in horror. Her trusted friend lay lifeless and bleeding on the ground.

"Take him!" Katari demanded, brutally tearing his weapon from the man's wound. Two Puma-warriors entered from the corridor and obediently dragged their murdered cohort from the tiny cell, a wide smear of blood following them.

Katari surveyed the Emissaries cowering before him. His power and insight had been compounding daily, and he felt stronger and more infallible than he ever had. His Helghul-brain whirred and cataloged information, always learning and plotting, spurred on by the ruthlessness of the Beast. He would not make the mistake of leaving witnesses in the future.

I told you! the Beast hissed.

"I should have killed you when I had the chance!" Katari spat at Sartaña, once again raising his bloody spear.

Inti let out a yelp as his rage exploded, eclipsing him. His reason and self-control disappeared in that moment, and he hurled the cool, hard stone still clenched between his rigid knuckles. In one swift motion, the young man propelled the rock at his father, who was only steps away, and it made a sickening impact with Katari's right temple as he launched his spear.

The leader was stunned. Helghul had never imagined the boy was capable of this, that his son, the spirit of Theron, could surprise him so completely. Katari's inner Beast yowled defiantly, and the eerie cry vibrated the chords of Katari's throat and echoed off the walls. He was filled with shock and rage, and his eyes flew wildly from Inti to Sartaña in disbelief. Pain seared his brain, and the first show of blood trickled from his ear. The hemorrhaging man grunted, slumped to his knees, and then fell facedown in the dirt, dead.

The black shadowed shine of Helghul lifted out of Katari, with the Beast threaded tightly through him. Inti and Sartaña couldn't see it. They saw only Sartaña's fingers wrapped around the unyielding wooden post sticking out of her belly. Katari's dead hands were empty; in his last moments, his spear had been launched.

The priestess looked at the spear protruding from her torso and thought of Amaru, her first son, who had died this same painful death. Inti dropped to her side. He had failed to stop Katari, and he was desperate to save Sartaña, though it was obvious that she was beyond hope.

I will never leave you, Sartaña thought, her Marcus-brain reaching out telepathically to Theron, but Inti could not hear.

"I was lied to . . . I didn't know," Inti said. Sartaña raised her weak hand to his lips, stopping his apologies. She didn't need them. She was grateful to be in his arms, thankful that Katari was dead and that he could no longer torment them. *Now we can stay in Stone-at-Center and rule together,* she thought, denying the gravity of her injuries.

With a whisper, Marcus was no longer in Inti's arms. He was no longer Sartaña. His perception changed, and Marcus was watching from above. His child—Inti—his soulmate, sat below him crying, with the dead shell of the High Priestess in his arms.

No! I can't leave. I won't go! Marcus thought. *Inti needs me. He's alone!*

Marcus's spirit had separated from Sartaña's devastated body and was slipping away, his shine pulled away from Theron's, but he struggled to stay.

Marcus was determined to reenter the body. He thrust himself back into Sartaña, but her lungs could no longer hold a breath, and her arrested heart would not cooperate. This vehicle was beyond repair, and his spirit could not restart it.

It was better to be out—free of the human struggle, pain, and separation. But Marcus resisted the comfort and connection, thinking only of Theron suffering alone on the floor of the putrid cell, surrounded by death.

Marcus couldn't hold on.

The Puma-warriors returned to the cell and were shocked to see Inti tenderly holding the murdered prisoner, and Katari murdered at their feet.

"Get him out!" Inti shouted, relieved that the Puma-warriors obeyed him.

The boy had not intended to kill his father. He had not intended anything at all. He had merely reacted. He had lost control and had followed an impulse so overwhelming that he was powerless to stop himself.

Inti heard his father's voice in his head: *"You will skin many monkeys in life. A ruler must endure much, to do what needs to be done,"* and he understood that *he* had done what needed to be done. Katari's words flooded back to him as the Puma-warriors dragged him away.

The warriors had been afraid to touch the tyrant but were surprised to lift him and find that he was a man, nothing more. He was only a shell, an empty sleeve, and the spirit that had inhabited Katari's body was gone—and with it, the largeness and terror of Helghul and the Beast.

Guilt, grief, relief—Inti was feeling all of it. The boy was overwhelmed by the abundance of emotions swirling within him. His parents were both gone. He was alone.

⋈ ⋈ ⋈

The citizens did not grieve for Katari, only for Sartaña. They had learned the truth of the priestess's incarceration and, happy to be free of their tyrant king, they had celebrated.

In a religious ceremony, Inti was crowned rightful High Priest and leader of Stone-at-Center and the surrounding lands. He led the people into an era of peace, prosperity, spirituality, and contentment. Without Katari pressing on him, Inti's compassion grew, and he saw that productivity and prosperity grew with it. He was wise and creative, and civilization advanced at Stone-at-Center, despite a continued worldwide descent into a darker Age. The Emissary was a light in a narrow pocket.

The stone carvings had played their part. Even two thousand years later, then called the Ica Stones, they would incite conversation, speculation, and wonder for those who heard of them.

Marcus's spirit had passed on, and though he didn't know it yet, it was he who was meant to counter Helghul. He would have to rise to the task, for he, too, had memories, and his life was inextricably linked to Helghul's. There were so many lifetimes to come, so many unexpected trials. Marcus was once more a spark in the grid, prepared to evaluate, be reborn, and to continue his struggle as an Emissary in the world of man.

Chapter 16

The Recyclables

Present day, Seattle, Washington

Quinn woke, choking back a sob. *Where am I? Who am I?* he thought, sitting up and trying to get his bearings. He'd had this dream before. He had been lying in Inti's arms and had been torn away. It was so real and fresh, as though they'd been together only moments before.

I will never leave you, he and Theron had promised each other back in Atitala, but it wasn't true. They *did* leave each other. Over and over they left one another, and over and over he searched.

There were much bigger stakes that had to be considered: Helghul, the Beast, and finding the Emerald Tablet, but it was difficult to focus on them when his loneliness and futility was overtaking him.

Quinn remembered the brave guard who had lost his life trying to help him in Stone-at-Center. He had known him many times since then.

There was a pounding at the door. Nine o'clock—only one person would show up unannounced, and Quinn smiled at the synchronicity. Nate, the very soul who had incarnated as his guard in his life as Sartaña, was eagerly waiting to be let in.

More than once, Nate's familiar spirit had given Marcus his only reprieve from bitter loneliness. Quinn was filled with affection and gratitude as he pulled on his robe and opened the door. Nate bounded into the room in a rush of excitement, with Starbucks coffee and muffins in hand.

"Dude! The investor came through. We got funding! We've been green-lit!" He paced the small apartment, unable to stand still. His hair, as always, was twisted in Bantu knots, and his black eyes sparkled with excitement.

"What are you talking about?" Quinn asked his friend, smiling. He loved Nate's constant enthusiasm.

Nate didn't reply. He was suddenly distracted, having noticed a colorful geometric painting Quinn had hung up the day before.

"That's new," he said. Nate noticed everything about everyone, and Quinn loved him for it.

"It's a mandala," Quinn said.

"I love that guy! Can you imagine being imprisoned like he was and still seeing good in the world? I didn't know he was an artist too."

"Not Nelson Mandela, a *man-da-la*. It's a model for understanding the universe," Quinn said, smirking. He had often wondered if the South African was an Emissary. "Are you going to tell me what has you so worked up or not?" Quinn asked, pulling Nate back on track.

"We start filming this week, and 'Seducer Producer' Oswald Zahn is going to fund the whole project!"

"That's incredible!"

Quinn had heard of Zahn—everyone had. He was a charming billionaire inventor/philanthropist who had recently turned movie producer. Zahn had a massive platform and a spotless reputation. He seemed to sincerely care about . . . everything. His nickname had been affectionately bestowed when he had first entered the movie industry, since no actor, producer, or director seemed capable of resisting his charm. Nate was just one more person who'd been won over.

"There's more. I met the girl of my dreams! Her name's Eden Anderson. She's directing the documentary."

"Wow, high praise . . . but she's your boss?"

"My cocreator, dude! She's brilliant and gorgeous—and, oh man, she knows her stuff. She's just . . . got it."

"And Sarah?" Quinn said, referring to Nate's long-term girl-friend and housemate. He felt bad for her. He liked Sarah—most of the time—but he also knew she and Nate had been bound to implode.

"I told her . . . this morning. And, yeah, we're done, which kinda leads me to my next question . . . ," Nate said, pausing.

Quinn raised his eyebrows and waited for what he knew was coming.

"Can I crash here for a while?"

"Naw, sorry man . . . ," Quinn began, and Nate's face fell with disappointment. "Yeah, of course you can!" the Emissary laughed. "Bring your stuff up, and, hey," he added as an afterthought, noticing the chaos of his kitchen counter, "I'm putting you in charge of the recyclables 'cause there's not room here for all of us. Either you, me, or that mountain of crap has to go!"

"Small price to pay, man. Thanks. It won't be for long. We'll be on location filming soon," Nate replied, giving him a hug and an excited clap on the back.

"Congratulations. I can't wait to meet your Eden," Quinn said, taking a sip of coffee, happy to have Nate's company.

My Eden, hmm, Nate mused, as he carried boxes of plastic, cardboard, and beer bottles out to his car and retrieved a duffel bag of clothes.

Seven hours and six phone calls from the crying ex-girlfriend later, most of Quinn's apartment was filled with steam from Nate's shower. Quinn didn't mind—he took a puff on a small roach and offered it to Nate, who refused with a frantic wave.

"You might want to have a pull just to calm your nerves a bit, buddy. You're pretty wired," Quinn said.

"I want to be sharp tonight. I don't want to miss half of what she says because I'm stuck in some stoner zone-out."

Ouch. Nate's guileless honesty hit a nerve, and Quinn was made conscious of his fuzzy state of mind. Nate was too distracted to notice and smoothed his hands down his blue silk shirt and shiny black pants. He checked his hair, which poked out in deliberate cones, in the mirror by the door as he left.

"Good luck!" Quinn called out, hoping for his friend's sake that he wouldn't see him again before noon the next day. He was tired and just wanted to tune out.

Quinn was asleep on the couch. Half a dozen empty beer bottles lined the coffee table, and he stirred when he heard Nate's key in the door. Quinn glanced at the time. Not good. An early night while on a date with the woman of your dreams did not bode well.

"Hey, man, what's going on?" Quinn asked groggily, smacking his dry lips as he sat up. He reached for a nearby beer to rinse his mouth but spit instead, blowing out the liquid, as he tongued the remnants of a joint he'd forgotten he'd drowned in the dregs of the bottle.

Disgusting! A new low, Emissary, Quinn thought, ashamed of himself. He dropped the roach back in the bottle and used a nearby tea towel to wipe up his spatter.

"Oh, man, I am so glad you don't have a date tonight," Nate started as he eagerly rounded the sofa.

"Yeah, me too," Quinn said wryly. Nate's candor was a test of Quinn's ability to shed his ego. He knew he was a mess, and the scene that had just unfolded only proved it.

"No, I mean, oh, I'm sorry. I—"

"Forget it! What's up?"

"I have kind of a big favor . . . well, I sorta made a promise, actually, but just say no if it's too much," Nate said.

"My wallet's on the table."

"No, man, I don't need your cash," Nate said.

"What, then?"

"Turns out, Eden's a huge fan of your blog. She's downstairs waiting in the car. I told her I could introduce you. She didn't want to put you on the spot, but she really wants to meet you. She thinks you can help with our project. Dude, we could all be working together!"

"Naw, not tonight, man. The place is a mess, and it smells like weed in here," Quinn said. He smacked his lips together. His mouth tasted like ash. *Disgusting!* he thought again.

"She's cool. She won't care. We'll pop in and leave real quick. Come on, I'll help you clean up," Nate said, transferring random cups and plates from the counter into the dishwasher at warp speed.

It was clear to Quinn as Nate bustled around the apartment tidying, that he was not going to take no for an answer. He shouldn't have to. Nate was a great pal, so it was the least Quinn could do. "Oh, what the hell . . . all right," Quinn said. "Light some incense. I gotta brush my teeth."

"Thanks, man, I owe you one," Nate said, happy to have good news to take back to his date.

"So it's going well?" Quinn called out from the bathroom.

"I'm in love, bro." Nate grinned, shoving jackets and shoes into the hall closet and forcing the door closed.

As Nate left to get Eden from the car, he bumped his shoulder on the doorway. He was literally bouncing off the walls, and Quinn laughed as he pushed some errant blades of grass under the living-room rug with his toe. He had never seen his friend so happy, and given Nate's cheerful temperament, that was saying a lot.

This Eden Anderson must truly be something special, Quinn thought, and his stomach fluttered, suddenly unusually nervous. The Emissary's hand flew to his messy hair, and he patted it down.

Chapter 17

Karma

Hearing Nate's easy laughter outside, Quinn stood waiting as the doorknob turned. Eden entered and the Emissary stared, suddenly frozen in place. His voice was trapped. There was a knot in his throat, and he was overcome. Unable to greet his guests, Quinn's mouth and eyebrows were contorting, and Nate was perplexed by the symphony of strange faces he was making.

Only something monumental could have affected Quinn so profoundly, and Eden was indeed worthy of that distinction. As the tiny brunette stepped out from behind Nate, she was almost completely obscured by the shine surrounding her. Quinn watched the indigo ribbons of energy pulsing from her. The color of her shine rippled in a graceful dance, joining with Marcus's and immersing him.

Delirium . . . joy . . . and profound connection overtook Quinn, and all of the oxygen in his lungs exhaled. He steadied himself, leaning on the sofa, his eyes transfixed.

Though Eden was a lovely-looking woman, Quinn could only see the soul that resided within her body. *It was his soulmate—Theron!* They had once again found each other. Quinn was filled with the most exquisite sensation.

She's found! Thank God! She's here! He closed his eyes, expressing his gratitude to the universe. He would have to tell Nate . . . but tell him what? Could he tell him everything? Thirteen thousand years of lifetimes, and all of it culminating in this tiny apartment? Living, dying, searching all the time for this soul, Nate's Eden Anderson?

Nate had helped the Emissary on his journey—many times. More than once he had sacrificed for Marcus. As Sartaña's guard, Nate's soul had reunited Marcus and Theron, and for doing so he had been torn from his body by Katari's vicious spear. Quinn owed him so much. Could he betray his ally? Could he make Nate understand?

Nate and Eden have only just met, Quinn rationalized to himself, but his conscience flooded him reminding him that Nate had already changed his life for Eden. He had left Sarah because of her, and was prepared to go on the road filming with her for the next three or four months or more.

Quinn's Marcus-brain was spinning, desperate to make it work. Could he figure out a way to be with Theron and not hurt Nate? Life was never simple, not for Emissaries—and not for soulmates. He recalled the times that he had found her and she had not been willing or able to accept him. It was difficult enough without his guilt and friendship with Nate further complicating matters!

Eden noticed that Quinn was frozen in place. He hadn't moved since she'd entered the room. He was odd. Surprisingly handsome, but odd. She hadn't expected that. Having followed his blog faithfully for years, she had often written comments and interacted with him online. In photos he had looked older, more professor-like, but from his writings, she had imagined him to be relaxed and funny. Here, in his living room, Quinn was nothing like she had expected, nor did he appear to be the charismatic mentor Nate had described. Based on Quinn's current stupor, Eden found him awkward, and he smelled like weed.

He just stood there, sort of hunched over and leaning, and though his mouth was moving, he said nothing. His hand had lifted like metal drawn to a magnet and just hung in the air, waiting for her to shake it. She was regretting putting the blogger on the spot.

"Hi. So glad to meet you," Eden said, stepping past Nate. She reached for Quinn's hand, and as she did so, he noticed a large Flower of Life tattoo on her forearm.

Electricity! When Theron and Marcus touched, the shine in the room redoubled. Only Quinn could see it, but Eden felt it tingle through her from head to toe. She felt the tremor, the magnetism, and the familiarity of all of their history running between them.

Finally, jolted to his senses, Quinn stood fully upright, placing his left hand over hers. His confidence was restored, and every cell in his body reached out to connect with her. He looked down into her green eyes and saw recognition and confusion in her face. Eden was drawn in and felt compelled by the powerful force that they shared. It was exciting, as if a doorway to some magical world had just opened.

Cherished images flashed through Eden's mind as she sought to understand her feelings: Alice finding Wonderland, Lucy entering Narnia through the wardrobe, Harry discovering the secret of Platform 9¾. She had none of Theron's life memories to call upon, but these were the references that best related to what Eden was experiencing, and they came to her in flashes at that moment.

"I'm in love, bro," Nate had said only moments earlier, so he watched Quinn and Eden with alarm. They were both transfixed. He felt compelled to step between them and intervene. They were still holding hands, and he knew he had to break the spell that was so clearly being cast.

Surely Nate would forgive the Emissary. Quinn sincerely hoped so, for as he held Eden's hand, he felt Theron's energy surging through him, revitalizing and reaffirming the love they shared. In that moment, only *she* mattered.

The soulmates had been reunited, but there was a higher cause beyond Nate's infatuation . . . and Marcus's connection to Theron. The Emissaries' lives were always brought together for a greater purpose.

What was the purpose this time?

For Nate, Quinn, and Eden, this reunion was a turning point . . . and it would change everything.

Bibliography

Carlson, Randolph, Randal Carlson Presents: The Great Year, http://www.youtube.com

Cruttenden, Walter, Cosmic Influence, podcast http://www.binary-institute.org

Cruttenden, Walter, The Great Year, Narrated by James Earl Jones, http://youtube.com

Dalai Lama XIV, His Holiness the, *How to Practice: The Way to a Meaningful Life* (Simon & Schuster, 2003)

De Santillana, Giorgio and Hertha Von Dechend, *Hamlet's Mill* (David R. Godine, Publisher, 1977)

The Grimerica Show, Podcast http://www.grimerica.ca

Hancock, Graham, *Fingerprints of the Gods* (New York, Three Rivers Press, 1995)

Hauk, Dennis William, *The Emerald Tablet: Alchemy of Personal Transformation* (New York, Penguin, 1999)

Jung, Carl Gustav and Roderick Main, *Jung on Synchronicity and the Paranormal* (London, Routledge, 1997)

Lanza, Robert, MD, with Bob Berman, *Biocentrism: How Life and Consciousness Are the Keys to Understanding the True Nature of the Universe* (Dallas, BenBella Press, 2009)

Laszlo, Ervin, *Science and the Akashic Field: An Integrated Theory of Everything* (Vermont, Inner Traditions, 1997)

Melchizedek, Drunvalo, *The Ancient Secrets of the Flower of Life Vol I, II* (Light Technology Publishing, 2000)

Newton, Michael, *Journey of Souls: World Case Studies of Life between Lives* (Llewellyn Publications, 1994)

Sheldrake, Rupert, *Morphic Resonance: The Nature of Formative Causation* 4th Edition (Park Street Press, 2009)

Stevenson, Ian, MD., *Children Who Remember Previous Lives A Question of Reincarnation* (McFarland Revised Edition, 2000)

Bibliography, Cont'd

Tarnas, Richard, *Cosmos and Psyche: Intimations of a New World View* (New York, Viking Penguin, 2007)

Tolle, Eckhart, *The Power of Now* (Vancouver, Namaste Publishing, 1999)

Yogananda, Paramahansa, *Autobiography of a Yogi* (Self-Realization Fellowship, 1971)

Yuketeswar, Sri Swami, *Holy Science* (University of Michigan, Self-Realization Fellowship, 1990)

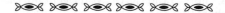

Book II
in
THE ONE GREAT YEAR SERIES
coming February 2019

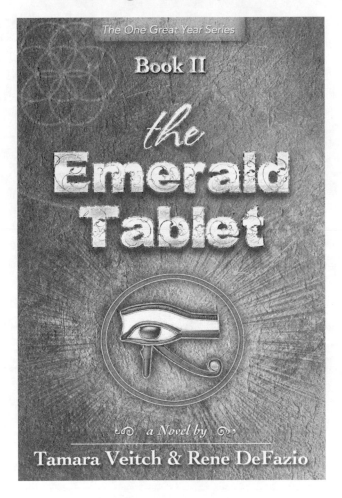

Please contact the authors via their website:
www.onegreatyear.com